Praise for previous mysteries by
Kate Kingsbury

"You'll enjoy your visit to the Pennyfoot Hotel."
—Hamilton Crane, author of *Miss Seeton's Finest Hour*

"Always most enjoyable." —*I Love a Mystery*

"Reminiscent of *Upstairs, Downstairs* . . . There are likable characters, period details, and a puzzle that kept me guessing until the end. A very enjoyable read."
—*Mystery News*

"Trust me, you will not be disappointed . . . Ms. Kingsbury has created a memorable series with delightful characters that can be enjoyed over and over again."
—*Myshelf.com*

"Delightful and charming." —Harriet Klausner

MORE MYSTERIES FROM THE
BERKLEY PUBLISHING GROUP...

SISTER FREVISSE MYSTERIES: Medieval mystery in the tradition of Ellis Peters . . .

by Margaret Frazer

THE NOVICE'S TALE	THE BISHOP'S TALE	THE REEVE'S TALE
THE OUTLAW'S TALE	THE BOY'S TALE	THE SQUIRE'S TALE
THE PRIORESS' TALE	THE MURDERER'S TALE	
THE SERVANT'S TALE	THE MAIDEN'S TALE	

PENNYFOOT HOTEL MYSTERIES: In Edwardian England, death takes a seaside holiday . . .

by Kate Kingsbury

ROOM WITH A CLUE	DO NOT DISTURB	CHIVALRY IS DEAD
SERVICE FOR TWO	EAT, DRINK, AND BE BURIED	RING FOR TOMB SERVICE
CHECK-OUT TIME	GROUNDS FOR MURDER	MAID TO MURDER
DEATH WITH RESERVATIONS	PAY THE PIPER	A BICYCLE BUILT FOR MURDER

GLYNIS TRYON MYSTERIES: The highly acclaimed series set in the early days of the women's rights movement . . . "Historically accurate and telling."—Sara Paretsky

by Miriam Grace Monfredo

SENECA FALLS INHERITANCE	THROUGH A GOLD EAGLE	MUST THE MAIDEN DIE
BLACKWATER SPIRITS	THE STALKING-HORSE	SISTERS OF CAIN
NORTH STAR CONSPIRACY		

MARK TWAIN MYSTERIES: "Adventurous . . . Replete with genuine tall tales from the great man himself."—*Mostly Murder*

by Peter J. Heck

DEATH ON THE MISSISSIPPI	THE GUILTY ABROAD
A CONNECTICUT YANKEE IN CRIMINAL COURT	THE MYSTERIOUS STRANGLER
THE PRINCE AND THE PROSECUTOR	

KAREN ROSE CERCONE: A stunning new historical mystery series featuring Detective Milo Kachigan and social worker Helen Sorby . . .

STEEL ASHES	BLOOD TRACKS	COAL BONES

A BICYCLE
BUILT FOR MURDER

KATE KINGSBURY

BERKLEY PRIME CRIME, NEW YORK

This is a work of fiction. Names, characters, places, and incidents either are the product of the author's imagination or are used fictitiously, and any resemblance to actual persons, living or dead, business establishments, events, or locales is entirely coincidental.

A BICYCLE BUILT FOR MURDER

A Berkley Prime Crime Book / published by arrangement with the author

PRINTING HISTORY
Berkley Prime Crime edition / February 2001

All rights reserved.
Copyright © 2001 by Doreen Roberts Hight.
This book, or parts thereof, may not be reproduced in any form without permission.
For information address: The Berkley Publishing Group, a division of Penguin Putnam Inc.,
375 Hudson Street, New York, New York 10014.

The Penguin Putnam Inc. World Wide Web site address is
http://www.penguinputnam.com

ISBN: 0-425-17856-0

Berkley Prime Crime Books are published
by The Berkley Publishing Group,
a division of Penguin Putnam Inc.,
375 Hudson Street, New York, New York 10014.
The name BERKLEY PRIME CRIME and the BERKLEY PRIME CRIME
design are trademarks belonging to Penguin Putnam Inc.

PRINTED IN THE UNITED STATES OF AMERICA

10 9 8 7 6 5 4 3 2 1

*This book is dedicated to the men,
women, and children of Great Britain
who kept the home fires burning during the
Second World War with unswerving humor,
unwavering courage, and the indispensable
cup of tea.*

And to Bill, who is and always has been my lifeline.

CHAPTER

❈ 1 ❈

The small formation of Spitfires swooped low over the eastern coastline. Their wings cast squat gray shadows across the wheat fields and the roofs of the tiny flint cottages perched on the cliffs below. The drone of their engines disturbed the quiet summer peace of the English countryside and raised the heads of cows grazing in farmer John Miller's pastures.

In the sloping main street of Sitting Marsh, housewives laden with bulging shopping bags paused to glance up at the aircraft. Reassured by the familiar blue-and-red circle painted on each wing, they continued trudging past the antiquated shops and narrow alleyways, their minds focusing once more on how to make a meal from the meager rations allowed them.

A little way out of town, in a twisting lane bordered by high hedgerows, a motorcycle wound its way around the bends. The woman riding it clung to a handlebar with one confident hand and blew a kiss as the planes passed overhead. Lady Elizabeth Hartleigh Compton, along with the entire population of the beleaguered British Isles, harbored a tremendous pride and gratitude for the valiant men who flew those illustrious machines.

Still clinging with one hand, she shaded her eyes against the sun to watch the aircraft disappear into a fluffy bank of cloud. Her inevitable ache of nostalgia was becoming easier to bear nowadays. It had been almost two years since both her parents had died during the blitz on London. She would never again see a plane fly overhead without thinking about her loss.

The next turn came up sooner than she expected, and even with the sidecar bouncing alongside her, she had to grab the handlebars and lean rather far to the left to make the corner. She really should pay attention, she reminded herself. To be tossed off the motorcycle would not only smart, but it was bound to ruin the yellow silk frock she wore. As it was, the necessity of having to tuck the skirt up under her knees tended to put creases in the worst places.

There were times when she doubted the wisdom of riding a motorcycle. She'd had to replace the ornamental daisies on her straw boater at least three times, thanks to the wind. Violet, her aging housekeeper, kept badgering her to buy a motorcar. Violet considered it improper for a thirty-one-year-old woman of Lady Elizabeth's standing to be riding a vulgar motorcycle in public when she should be driven around in a Daimler. Violet was very good at suggesting ways to spend money. The trouble was, there was very little money to spend. Certainly not enough to lavish on a motorcar, let alone a chauffeur.

Elizabeth lowered her chin as a salty gust of east wind nearly lifted her hat from her head despite the anchors of pins and the wide elastic band. Actually she rather enjoyed riding a motorcycle. It gave one a sense of utter freedom. Much like flying, she supposed. Not that she'd ever flown. Still, she could well imagine how it must feel.

At any rate, she knew very well that when she roared into town on her noisy steed, she commanded attention. If there was one thing Elizabeth considered important above all others, it was the ability to command attention. It was the only way to get things done.

Having so justified her choice of transportation, she chugged and sputtered up the hill toward the long drive-way that would take her home to the Manor House. She had about a half mile to go when a few yards down the road a woman appeared at a white, latticed garden gate and frantically waved a large handkerchief at her.

Even at that distance, Elizabeth could tell that Winnie Pierce was distraught about something. Winnie's family had been tenants of the Wellsborough estate for as long as Elizabeth could remember. When she'd inherited the Manor House upon the death of her parents, she'd also inherited the cottages on the vast acres that went with it. Which was just as well, since her miserable ex-husband had gambled away every penny of her inheritance. The rent from those cottages was the only thing standing between herself and abject poverty.

Not that the tenants knew that, of course. It might weaken her authority if the residents of Sitting Marsh knew their chief adviser and protector was struggling to keep the Manor House and all its holdings afloat in a sea of debts.

Elizabeth was well aware that the seventeenth-century Jacobean mansion, with its warm brick walls and towering windows, was a symbol of stability in a world gone mad. The imposing ancestral home visibly dominated the rural landscape, and the villagers looked upon those ancient walls as proof that the Old World still existed, and would go on existing, long after the Germans and their vicious Luftwaffe had done their worst.

Symbols as powerful as that had to be maintained, no matter the cost. She owed it to her people and to her family, whose traditions and heritage must be upheld. The residents of Sitting Marsh always came first. It was as simple as that.

Which was why she braked to a sudden stop in front of Winnie Pierce at great risk to her perilous control of the machine. The maneuver pitched her forward, and she bumped her chin painfully on the handlebar. She ran a tongue over her teeth to make sure they were all intact before climbing off as gracefully as one could manage under the circumstances.

Winnie flapped her apron up and down in front of her round face, which glowed like a ripe tomato. She smelled faintly of onions and garlic, and a smudge of flour adorned her left cheek.

Elizabeth immediately felt hungry. Having sampled the results of some of Winnie's delectable culinary skills in the past, she rather hoped her tenant would invite her to the midday meal. Violet did her best, but cooking was not one of her greatest achievements, and now that everything was rationed, the housekeeper's offerings were becoming decidedly insipid.

"I'm so sorry, Lady Elizabeth," Winnie said breathlessly. "I know I shouldn't have stopped you, but I've been so worried. I'm at my wits' end, really I am."

Concerned by the poor woman's obvious agitation, Elizabeth patted her plump shoulder. "It's quite all right, Winnie. Just calm down and tell me what's the matter."

"Well, I don't rightly know, m'm. It's Beryl, you see."

Elizabeth took a moment to smooth out the folds in her skirt. Beryl was Winnie's sixteen-year-old daughter, an only child and thoroughly spoiled. Beryl's promiscuous activities were the hot topic of the town and a source of great worry for her poor parents. Elizabeth had taken it upon herself to talk some sense into the child, whose overdeveloped attributes drew attention from the boys like flies to a dustbin. Beryl had listened politely and completely ignored the proffered counsel.

Half afraid to ask, Elizabeth murmured, "I do hope she isn't sick?"

"Oh, no, m'm. At least, I don't think so."

To Elizabeth's dismay, the poor woman burst into tears. It was a moment or two before she'd sufficiently recovered herself enough to speak. "She's missing, m'm. She's been gone since Sunday. That's two whole days."

The news appeared worse than Elizabeth had anticipated. But then, Beryl was quite capable of causing her mother distress simply on a whim. "Perhaps she's hiding out with a friend somewhere," she said soothingly. "Are any of her clothes missing? Did you have an argument with her?"

"No, nothing like that." Winnie uttered a shuddering sigh accompanied by a loud sniff, but at least she seemed to have stopped crying for the moment. "The last time I saw her, which was Saturday afternoon, she went out of here as happy as a lark. Said she was going to meet Evan. Only Evan says she never turned up."

Elizabeth raised her eyebrows. "She's still going out with Evan? I thought that had finished weeks ago."

Winnie shook her head. "It's been on again, off again since then, but Beryl seemed really keen to see him on Saturday. She even left early. Evan said they weren't supposed to meet until seven o'clock, but Beryl left here about half past five."

"Did she say where she was meeting him?"

"Never said a word. You know our Beryl. I'm surprised she even told me that much. But Evan told me they'd arranged to meet outside the Tudor Arms. He was going to take her to the dance in North Horsham."

"What did he do when she didn't arrive?"

"Went off in a huff, that's what. Never even bothered to find out what happened to her. I had to go down to the farm on Sunday night and ask if he'd seen her. That's when I found out she hadn't turned up." Winnie twisted her hands in her apron. "Wherever she went on Saturday night, it wasn't with Evan. I didn't see her come in, but I heard her all right. I was half asleep, but I called out to her. She never answered me, little bugger."

"Did she say anything the next morning?"

Winnie shook her head. "She was gone by the time I got up. Never made her bed before she went out neither. Strange, really. Our Beryl never can get up in the mornings without me yelling up the stairs until I'm hoarse. Whatever got her out of the house that early on a Sunday must have been really important."

It was Elizabeth's considered opinion that Beryl was allowed far too much freedom for a young girl, which was bound to have adverse effects. She refrained from voicing the sentiment, however, and tried to be practical about the problem. "Have you had a word with George? He might have seen her on his rounds."

She actually saw Winnie's face turn white. "The police? Oh, no, m'm, I couldn't. I don't want to get my Beryl into trouble. Not more than what she is already, anyhow."

As far as George Dalrymple was concerned, Elizabeth

didn't really think of him as being "the police." Along with his colleague, Sid Goffin, he'd been brought out of retirement when the younger, and considerably more efficient, constables had been called up for the army.

George had been very happy pottering around his little garden all day and had not taken kindly to being hauled away from his well-earned peaceful existence. Faced with the demand to do something for the war effort, however, he'd been powerless to refuse. His services were given grudgingly, at best. And as infrequently as he could manage.

"I don't think George would make trouble for Beryl," Elizabeth assured Winnie.

"Maybe not," Winnie said firmly, "but I don't want to do anything that might hurt my Beryl's reputation."

It was on the tip of Elizabeth's tongue to point out that it was a tad too late to worry about the child's reputation. She held her silence while Winnie stared down the road as if expecting to see her errant offspring appear at any minute.

"If only Stan was here," Winnie murmured unhappily. "He always knew how to handle our Beryl. She's been such a handful since he left to join the navy. A young girl needs a father around, that's what I always say."

At a loss for any brilliant suggestions, Elizabeth shook her head. "It's a hard time for all of us. Wartime demands sacrifices from all of us, and we just have to make the best of it, that's all."

"Yes, m'm." Winnie gave a loud sniff. "I wouldn't be surprised if all this didn't have something to do with them Yanks."

Elizabeth blinked. "The war? Oh, I don't think the Americans had anything to do with it. It's Hitler's fault. He started it all."

Winnie looked startled. "No, m'm. I mean Beryl disappearing like that. She's always talking about the Yanks and going to the base. I've strictly forbidden it, of course. A young girl of her age wouldn't stand a chance out there with all them barbarians, from what I've heard. It's no wonder girls get a bad name if they're seen talking to 'em. I wouldn't let my child near 'em."

Elizabeth's sense of justice could not let that go by without some form of protest. "I'm sure they're not as bad as people like to make out. They are young men, after all, who have come very far from home to help fight this dreadful war, and we should be grateful for their presence here."

Winnie gave her a sly look. "Would *you* go out with one, m'm?"

Appalled by the very idea, Elizabeth lifted her chin. "Certainly not."

Winnie nodded. "That's what I thought. All I'm saying is that Sitting Marsh hasn't been the same since they moved into that airport. What with all them girls coming in from the town, and the Land Army girls elbowing them out the way, there's no room in the Tudor Arms anymore for those what live here. The pub's always full of strangers. Noisy ones at that." She glanced at Elizabeth out the corner of her eye. "At least, that's what they tell me," she added hurriedly. "But then, as you say, it's wartime and we have to make the best of things."

"Indeed. Though it might be an idea to ask Ted Wilkins if he's seen Beryl," Elizabeth suggested. "After all, he owns the pub, and he's there all the time. He might be able to help."

"I suppose so." Winnie stared down the road again. "I just wish Stan was here. He's so much better at this than I am."

Seeing Winnie's forlorn expression, Elizabeth was prompted to offer rashly, "Would you like me to see what I can do?"

She was immediately rewarded by the other woman's expression of relieved gratitude. "Oh, would you, m'm? I hate to ask, really I do, but I don't know which way to turn. I would be ever so grateful if you could find out where she is for me."

"Well, I can't promise anything," Elizabeth said quickly, "but I will do what I can. Please try not to worry. I'm sure she's just having a game with you."

"If she is, I'll box her blinking ears when she gets home," Winnie threatened darkly. "Thank you so much, Lady Elizabeth." She glanced at her front door. "Would you like to come in for a nice cup of tea?"

"Oh, that's very kind of you." Elizabeth gazed longingly up the garden path. Winnie's cottage beckoned with an air of comfort and cozy serenity rarely found in the vast, empty rooms and hallways of the Manor House. The tiny latticed windows, tucked beneath the thickly thatched roof and discreetly covered with white net curtains, were almost hidden behind masses of yellow marigolds burgeoning from the window boxes.

Daisies, hollyhocks, and Canterbury bells lined the pebble path, their graceful heads nodding in the sea breeze, enticing her to wander past their fragrance to the cozy warmth of Winnie's kitchen.

With a sigh Elizabeth resisted the impulse to take Winnie up on her offer. "I really should be getting back. Violet worries so much when I'm out on the motorcycle. She's convinced I'm going to meet with some dreadful calamity on the road."

Winnie eyed the gleaming red machine with a dubious look on her face. "If you don't mind my saying so, it *is* rather dangerous for a woman to ride one of those things. Not that it's any of my business, of course. It's just that I wouldn't want anything bad to happen to you. I don't know what Sitting Marsh would do without you, m'm. Really I don't. After losing Lord and Lady Wellsborough like that and all. There's been an Earl of Wellsborough for as long as Sitting Marsh has been in existence. It just doesn't seem right not to have one anymore."

Elizabeth felt a pang of resentment. "Yes, well, it's unfortunate that women can't inherit an earldom. I'm sure my father would have preferred a son to whom he could hand down the title, but we can't all have everything we want."

Winnie's face flushed with dismay. "Oh, no, m'm, I didn't mean anything by it, really I didn't. You've done wonders for the village, really you have. There isn't one person living in Sitting Marsh who doesn't regard you with the highest respect and admiration. We all love you dearly, Lady Elizabeth. Every last one of us. Really."

Appeased by this outburst, Elizabeth relented. She was well aware that her sensitivity stemmed not so much from Winnie's remark or, for that matter, a lack of title, but from the fact that her mother had never been truly accepted by the villagers.

Elizabeth's mother, Mavis, had been nothing more than a fifteen-year-old kitchen maid when she'd caught the eye of Lord Hartleigh. He'd eventually married her, much to the horror of the villagers and Nigel Hartleigh's father, the Earl of Wellsborough.

Although Mavis had quickly learned the customs and manners of an aristocrat and had looked every inch the part, her lack of family breeding had remained a barrier between her and society for the rest of her short life.

Despite the fact that no mention of Elizabeth's diverse

heritage had ever been uttered by anyone in Sitting Marsh, she was constantly aware that the disparity remained in her background and no doubt would be handed down to future generations, if there were to be any.

The way things looked now, there was plenty of room for doubt, she reminded herself as she continued on her way, having assured Winnie that no offense had been taken.

Her marriage to Harry Compton had lasted less than nine years. Fortunately, as it turned out, there had been no child from that marriage, though in weaker moments Elizabeth found herself dealing with a deep sense of missing something important in her life. Her experiences with her ex-husband, however, had left her with a strong aversion to romantic entanglements and a profound mistrust of men in general.

Although her sense of fair play cautioned her that to lump all men into one odious category was not exactly cricket, her outrage and contempt over Harry's betrayal had deeply wounded her, and this was one area where she was simply unable to rationalize.

If Beryl had any sense, she'd stay away from men altogether, Elizabeth thought sourly as she pulled up at the wrought-iron gates that opened onto the Manor House grounds. She only hoped the poor girl hadn't run off with someone the way she had done so herself ten years ago. If so, more than likely Beryl would live to regret it.

Her dark thoughts scattered as she rode up the long driveway to the house. Passing through the wooded land with its myriad wildlife on either side of her always brought her a sense of peace, even in these turbulent times.

Fortunately, London and the major cities were too far away for Sitting Marsh to suffer the horrors of the bombing—so far, at least. But even the petty annoyances and inconveniences of wartime seemed to fade into insignificance whenever Elizabeth saw the red brick walls of the Manor House coming into view around the tree-lined bend.

How she loved this sprawling, ancient mansion, in spite of its empty rooms, the plumbing problems, the leaking roofs, and drafty windows. This was her home, her heritage. This was what she lived for, worked for, prayed for with every fiber of her being.

Who needed a man, she asked herself, her spirits rising as she sputtered to a stop in front of gleaming white marble steps. Who needed a man when she had all this? This was her life: these stately grounds and proud, magnificent walls with their centuries of history locked behind them. This was who she was and always would be: Lady Elizabeth Hartleigh Compton, daughter of the Earl and Countess of Wellsborough. She was home.

It was only then that she noticed the vehicle parked on the other side of the circular driveway. It seemed she had a visitor. Moreover, by the looks of the dilapidated jeep resting against her flowerbed, the intruder was one of that much-maligned species, an American. Now, what on earth would an American be doing at the Manor House?

Feeling a deep sense of foreboding, Elizabeth hurried up the steps of her ancestral home and prepared herself for the worst.

CHAPTER

❧ 2 ❧

The heavy oak door opened slowly to Elizabeth's urgent summons on the clanging bell. Many times she'd thought about replacing the historical pull bell with a modern electric buzzer. Thank heavens her father had the foresight to have electricity installed in the house while there was still money to pay for it.

The bell, however, belonged to an era long since gone, and Elizabeth was reluctant to part with one of the fast-vanishing remnants of those idealistic times. She often thought how wonderful it must have been to live in an age when women were cherished and pampered.

Nowadays women were expected to act like men, taking the place of their male counterparts in factories, shops, and farms all over the country. Women wore trousers, drove lorries, dug ditches, and built airplanes. Sometimes it was hard to tell they were women at all.

While she might ride a motorcycle, Elizabeth assured

13

herself, she would never be seen in public without a decent frock and a hat—albeit at great inconvenience to herself at times. Still, appearances had to be kept up. Always a lady, as her mother had reminded her again and again.

The door finally opened wide enough for her to step inside the wide entrance hall, though the person behind it remained hidden. The familiar smell of furniture polish mingled with the fragrance of freshly picked roses, reminding her sharply of her mother.

Shaking off the painful twinge, Elizabeth put one foot on the embroidered welcome mat protecting the polished parquet floor and inquired cautiously, "Martin?"

She heard a faint scuffle of feet, and Martin's crinkled face appeared from behind the door. "Goodness gracious, madam! Whatever are you doing out there without an escort?"

Elizabeth sighed. Martin had been with the family since before the turn of the century. He had long ago outlived his usefulness as a butler, though he was completely unaware of that fact, thanks to Elizabeth's determination to give the doddery old man a home for as long as he needed one.

She, and for the most part Violet, too, turned a blind eye to his faltering memory and occasional bouts of dementia. Although his spirit remained as willing as ever, his body was often too weak to comply, and Elizabeth gamely undertook his duties, while making every effort to convince the senile gentleman that he was still in full possession of his faculties.

That wasn't always as simple as it sounded, considering that a large amount of the time, Martin lived in the past, when he and the modern world were still in their guileless youth.

She gave him a fond smile and gently closed the door with his hand still clinging stubbornly to the ornate brass handle. "Thank you, Martin. I see we have a visitor."

"We do?" Martin blinked owlishly at her over the thin gold rims of his glasses. He never could get the hang of looking through them, and constantly blundered into whatever obstacle happened to be in his path.

"The jeep," Elizabeth said helpfully. "It looks like an American vehicle."

"Does it really?" Martin shook his head. His white hair had thinned until just a few wisps remained, which he insisted on having trimmed every week or so, at great risk of losing what little hair he had left. Violet pretended to snip at the strands for him until he was satisfied that he looked respectable.

Elizabeth tried again. "Did you happen to see the driver of the jeep?"

Martin's watery blue eyes peered anxiously at her. "Perhaps if madam could enlighten me as to the nature of a jeep? I'm not familiar with that term."

"It's a motor vehicle, Martin. You know, like a carriage without a horse."

Martin nodded. "Ah, one of those newfangled contraptions. I trust you are not contemplating setting foot in one of those death machines?"

"Of course not, Martin."

"I should certainly hope not. Your father would turn in his grave."

"No doubt." Elizabeth glanced at the door on her left, which stood slightly ajar. "Martin, would you please ask Violet to send some tea and sandwiches to the library? Is Polly still here?"

"I think so, madam. I'll see to it right away." Martin inclined his head, then twisted around until he was facing toward the steps that led to the kitchen. He shuffled a few steps, then halted.

Elizabeth waited until he'd maneuvered his body so that he was facing her again, then asked gently, "What is it, Martin?"

He shuffled back toward her and whispered loudly, "You can't go in the library, madam. There's a gentleman in there."

"That's quite all right, Martin. I'll use the utmost caution. Besides, Polly will be along any moment with the sandwiches, all right?"

"Ah, yes. Sandwiches. I'll have her bring them right away."

"And tea, Martin." She glanced again at the library door. "Perhaps you should have her bring some sherry, as well."

Martin shuffled off, muttering to himself and repeating his mission over and over as he climbed painfully down the stairs.

Elizabeth waited until he'd reached the bottom safely, then headed for the library.

The visitor had his back to her when she silently entered the quiet room. He was studying the rows of books—her father's books—that lined the shelves from floor to ceiling. Her father had been a great reader and had collected just about every piece of classical literature published.

Elizabeth took advantage of the moment to study the stranger. He wore the forest green uniform of an American air force pilot, which was becoming a familiar sight in Sitting Marsh. His hands were clasped behind his back, and his broad shoulders were squared in a typical military stance.

She must have made some slight sound, as he turned

sharply and impaled her with eyes so light blue they appeared to have little color at all. The contrast against his leathery, sunburned skin was startling. When he swept off his cap, she saw streaks of blond in his light brown hair. This was a man who lived outdoors in the hot sun. How he must miss that here in the cool mists of England.

"Good afternoon," she said, surprised to hear the tremor in her voice. She felt a little intimidated by the man's presence, and it wasn't a feeling to which she was accustomed. It had to be the uniform. This was the closest she'd been to an American, and some of the wild tales she'd heard about them gleefully circulated in her head.

"Ma'am." He offered his hand; then, as if unsure of the gesture, he withdrew it again. "Major Monroe, United States Air Force. I'm here to see the owner of this establishment."

He had a deep burr of an accent that made her think of cowboys and wide-open plains. She nodded warily. "That would be me."

He stared at her for so long she wondered if she had mud all over her face. Riding a motorcycle had more than one disadvantage. She raised her hands to her hat, just to reassure herself it was still anchored to her hair and not hanging down her back as had been known to happen in the past.

"*You're* Lady Wellsborough?" he said at last, sounding utterly amazed.

"Lady Elizabeth actually," she said pleasantly. "There is no Lady Wellsborough."

Now he looked confused. "But I was told that Lady Wellsborough owned this place."

"Then you were misinformed. Lady Wellsborough was my mother. She was married to Lord Wellsborough, my father, who was the Earl of Wellsborough. I, however, am known as Lady Elizabeth. It all has to do with the inheritance of titles, which is terribly biased in favor of men and completely outdated as far as I'm concerned. In any case, it would take far too long to explain it all now."

"Yes, ma'am." For a moment he seemed to struggle with the information she'd given him, then apparently gave up. His gaze flicked over her. "I was kind of expecting someone a lot older."

"Sorry to disappoint you. How may I be of service, Major Monroe? That *is* what one calls you, isn't it? I'm not familiar with American customs. I wasn't aware that you had majors in the air force."

"Army Air Force, ma'am. Though I'd rather you called me Earl."

She lifted her chin, sensing he was making fun of her. "We usually reserve that title for gentlemen of nobility."

His laugh took her by surprise. "No, ma'am. That's my name. Earl Monroe. At least, that's what it says on my birth certificate."

"Oh, I see." Now she felt foolish. And annoyed at him for making her so. "Excuse me. I've never heard of anyone being called Earl before."

"Well, I've never met the daughter of one before, so I reckon that makes us even. So, what do I call the daughter of an earl?"

"As I've already told you, I'm known as Lady Elizabeth."

His eyes crinkled at the corners. "All the time?"

"All the time," Elizabeth said firmly.

He nodded, then swept a long glance around the library, taking in the high, ornate ceiling carved centuries ago, the majestic windows with their imposing view of the grounds, the vast open fireplace and Italian marble mantelpiece, right down to the deep blue Axminster carpet. "Quite a palace you have here."

Elizabeth smiled, pleased by his warm admiration of her treasured domain. "Thank you, but it's not a palace. It's a mansion."

"What's the difference?"

She wasn't sure, but she was reluctant to let him know that. "In England, the word palace usually refers to the home of royalty." That sounded right, anyway.

"And you're not?"

"Royalty? Not exactly. Nobility, I suppose, would describe it more accurately."

"Could I look around?"

"Why, of course! I—" A faint tap on the door interrupted her. The door opened, and a young girl edged in, carrying a large tray.

Elizabeth was happy to see Polly wearing a dress. She was only a part-time maid and lately had taken to wearing trousers to work, despite Elizabeth's protests. Today she'd pinned up her long, dark hair into a tight coil circling around her head. No doubt the latest fashion of some film star garnered from a motion picture magazine. "You can put the tray down there, Polly," Elizabeth said, indicating a small table in the bay window.

Polly gaped at the American as she carried the tray past him and dumped it rather heavily on the table. Still staring at him, she backed away a few steps, then turned and rushed from the room.

Elizabeth sighed. "When I was a child, a maid would never have dared to behave in such an atrocious manner. But then, it's almost impossible to get decent help these days." She started toward the table. "May I offer you a glass of sherry and a sandwich?"

"Oh, that's real kind of you, ma'am, but I have to get back to the base."

"Oh." Somewhat nonplussed, she turned to face him. "In that case, you had better tell me why you are here."

"Yes, ma'am." Earl Monroe stared down at the cap he was twisting in his hands.

Elizabeth felt a small jump of apprehension when she realized the American was reluctant to give her the reason for his visit. Somehow she didn't think it was simply idle curiosity that had brought him to the Manor House. She waited, heart thumping, for him to raise his head.

"I'm sorry, ma'am," he said finally. "I've been ordered to inform you that your home is being requisitioned to house American officers for an unknown period of time."

It took her a full ten seconds to comprehend his words. In the long silence that followed his statement, she heard quite clearly the loud tick of the grandfather clock in the hallway, and somewhere downstairs a door slammed. No doubt Polly on her way out.

American officers. Here, in one of the most cherished stately homes in England? "That's impossible," she said bluntly.

Major Monroe at least had the grace to look unhappy. "I reckon there isn't much any of us can do about it, ma'am. The air base isn't big enough to accommodate the men as well as the officers. Yours is the only establishment within miles that would suit our purposes."

"Well, we'll see about that. I'll call Whitehall. I'll call the prime minister. I'll call the palace. This is an outrage." She stared in consternation as Monroe tucked his fingers into his breast pocket and withdrew a slip of paper.

"I reckon you should take a peek at this, ma'am."

The paper trembled in her fingers when she scanned

the typewritten lines. There was no mistake. The dictate bore the stamp of the War Office.

For a long moment she struggled with her resentment, then reminded herself, as she had so many times, that there was a war on. Just last year the government had passed a National Service Act, conscripting women between the ages of twenty and thirty for either military or vital war purposes.

There were rumors that the limit would be raised to fifty years of age before too long. It was only a matter of time. She might as well start doing her bit right now. At least she'd be allowed to stay in her own home. But she didn't have to like it.

She turned to gaze out the window, appalled at the thought of her home being overrun by the hooligans who had become the terror of the town. "When will this take place?"

He must have heard the tremor in her voice. "Next week, ma'am. I'm real sorry we have to do this, but I swear to you, they're all swell guys. They'll keep out of your way as much as possible, and they'll do their best not to disrupt the household. I'll see to it myself."

"Thank you, Major Monroe," Elizabeth murmured, "but I think we both know that life at the Manor House will be somewhat different for a while."

"Yes, ma'am. Let's just hope it won't be for too long."

"Amen." She headed for the door, saying over her shoulder, "I'd better show you around, I suppose. I'm sure you have to report back to your superiors."

She gave him a quick tour of the house, showing him only what she deemed necessary. All the time she mechanically answered questions, while her mind wrestled with the complexities of housing a number of men in her home. Violet would have a fit. Polly would probably walk out. God knows how Martin would deal with all this.

She showed Earl Monroe the east wing, which had the most adjacent rooms, though the plumbing in the single bathroom could cause some problems. Something she'd have to face when the men arrived. No one had used that part of the house since her parents had died.

The American kept stopping in the great hall to admire the long rows of her ancestors' portraits hanging on the walls. It intrigued her that the man would so readily give up lunch yet linger to examine a few paintings.

By the time he left, thanking her profusely for her cooperation, she felt exhausted. Now she had to face Violet, which she wasn't looking forward to at all. She went back to the library, poured herself a large sherry, and ate two of the sandwiches before picking up the tray to carry it back to the kitchen.

Violet was seated in her favorite spot by the enormous open fireplace when Elizabeth charged through the door. She dropped the magazine she was reading and leapt to her feet, snatching the tray from Elizabeth's hands before she could utter a word.

In spite of a healthy appetite, Violet's body was thin and wiry, and with her frizzy gray hair standing on end more often than not, together with the ill-fitting clothes she insisted on wearing, she looked a little like a weathered scarecrow. Her features were pinched, her mouth small and puckered, and she had a habit of tilting her head onto one shoulder when she talked, often reminding Elizabeth of an inquisitive sparrow.

"I could have got this later," she said crossly. "Of course, if Polly hadn't shot off early, she could have brought it back. Lazy cow. I sometimes wonder why she bothers to come here at all. Taking money under false pretenses, that's what she does."

Elizabeth sank into a chair next to the large wooden table that had dominated the kitchen for more than a hundred years. She buried her face in her hands and tried to calm her churning thoughts.

"What's wrong, Lizzie? Got a headache, have you?"

Elizabeth lowered her hands again. Violet was the only person in the world, besides her parents, who was allowed to call her by her childhood name. Although she knew that some of the villagers referred to her as Lady Liza, no one had ever called her that to her face. To all intents and purposes, she had always been, and always would be, Lady Elizabeth. And that included Major Earl Monroe and his merry band of men.

"Violet," she said wearily, "I'm afraid I have some rather disturbing news."

"Oh, Gawd." Violet clutched her chest. "Not someone been killed?"

"No, no, nothing like that." For a moment a vision of Beryl's perky face sprang to mind. Elizabeth quickly shook off the image. "No, it's the American air force."

"Ah." Violet's chin bobbed up and down. "Polly told me about him. Said he was really handsome."

Elizabeth looked her straight in the eye. "Really? I can't say I noticed."

"Well, you know Polly. She thinks anything in trousers is handsome. Course, now that women are wearing them, too, I suppose I can't say that no more. Anyhow, what did he want?"

"He wants us to house some of the officers from the base."

Violet's voice rose to squeak. "Americans? In here? I hope you told him to bugger off."

"It's wartime, Violet. We all have to make sacrifices. I told him we'd do what we could to help out." She hoped that Violet would accept the news more easily if she didn't know it had been a direct order.

"Why'd they have to pick here? What's wrong with putting them up at the pub or the cricket pavilion? Now that the men are all gone, the clubhouse is empty. No one ever uses it now, except for youngsters looking for trouble." Violet got a faraway look in her eyes. "I really miss them cricket matches. Made a nice afternoon out, it did."

Elizabeth silently agreed. "The cricket pavilion doesn't have bathing facilities. The Manor House really is the only place available for those men. I don't see how we can refuse."

The housekeeper still looked disgruntled. "I hope I don't have to cook for that lot. What do Americans eat, anyhow? Probably want me to kill a cow for them, more'n likely. Do they know we've got rationing? How are we supposed to feed all of them?"

"I daresay they will make their own arrangements for meals," Elizabeth said, hoping for the best. "In any case, I have something more important to worry about right now. I saw Winnie Pierce on my way back home. She tells me Beryl has been missing for two days. I promised her I'd do what I can to find out where she is."

"Oh, crikey, that was probably a mistake. You know what Beryl Pierce is like. You could be walking into a whole lot of trouble, there."

Elizabeth heaved yet another sigh. She hated to admit it, but something told her that Violet was absolutely right. This was not turning out to be one of her better days.

CHAPTER

❀ 3 ❀

"We really should put up new curtains at these windows," Elizabeth said later that afternoon. "These are so threadbare they'll fall apart before too long. Especially now that they'll be pulled back and forth every day."

"No one's going to notice them with the blackout blinds under them," Violet muttered. "They make any kind of curtains look ugly."

Elizabeth gloomily agreed. She and Violet were standing in the master suite of the east wing, trying to decide what renovations were needed and what she could afford. The gap between the two specifics seemed insurmountable.

Scrutinizing the faded wallpaper, with its oblique design of peasant girls gathering flowers in what appeared to be an endless meadow, she murmured, "This pattern seems awfully inappropriate for military quarters. The paper seemed so glamorous when Mother picked it out, but now it reminds me of a bordello in Paris."

Violet's sparse eyebrows arched in horror. "When did you ever see one of those places?"

"Never, though at times I feel like running off to one. What are we going to do with these walls? We simply don't have time, let alone the money, to redecorate now."

"If you ask me, you're worrying far too much." Violet waved an arm at the walls. "These men are used to army barracks. This house will seem like blessed paradise compared to that. Besides, they'll have so much stuff on the walls they won't even notice the paper."

"But the curtains—"

"What are you worrying about curtains for? We'll just take them down."

"We can't do that. Those black blinds are so awful. We need something to brighten up the windows."

"From what I hear in the village, the Yanks aren't too fussy about anything like that. You should hear what that Rita Crumm says about—"

"I'd rather not." Aware that she'd butted in rather rudely, Elizabeth added, "I really think we should discourage gossip as much as possible under the circumstances. Especially from Rita Crumm. She has such a beastly habit of exaggerating everything she hears. I'm sure there will be enough talk once everyone discovers we are entertaining Americans as our guests."

"Oh, crikey, I can hear them now." Violet cocked her head to her shoulder. "You know, Lizzie, it's not very good for your reputation—alone in this house with a bunch of rowdy Americans. What if one of them gets saucy?"

Elizabeth smiled. "I'm quite sure they'll all be far too

busy fighting the war to pay attention to me. Besides, I'm a good deal older than most of them."

"I don't know about that." Violet sent her a sly look from the corner of her eye. "What about that major, then? I bet he's older than you."

Elizabeth reached out for a fold of the heavy damask curtain and gave it a shake. "Major Monroe has to set an example to the rest of the men. I'm quite sure he'll be the epitome of decorum."

Violet sniffed. "From what I've heard, those Yanks don't know the meaning of the word. I can see trouble coming, especially with young Polly in the house. Without a chaperone we three women will be at their mercy."

"We do have a chaperone. We have Martin."

Violet's derisive laugh echoed hollowly in the vast, empty room. "Fat lot of good he'd be. By the time he knew what was going on, one of those Yanks could have had his way with all three of us."

Elizabeth turned sharply. "That's enough, Violet. I don't believe in looking for trouble. I prefer to give Major Monroe and his men the benefit of the doubt and assume they are all perfect gentlemen."

"All I'm saying is that it doesn't hurt to be on guard. After all—"

Elizabeth raised her hand, effectively cutting off Violet's next words. "Isn't that the telephone ringing?"

Violet hurried over to the door. "I hope whoever it is hangs on until I get there. If you're going to open up this wing again, we should have another extension put in here. Otherwise we'll be running ourselves ragged with messages for them Yanks."

She disappeared through the door, and Elizabeth let out her breath in a long sigh. So many things to take care of, and the Americans hadn't even moved in yet. Heaven help them all when that fateful day arrived. Right now the least of her worries was unwanted advances from the men. She'd had lots of practice defusing that sort of situation. If she couldn't keep a few boisterous Americans in their place, then she wasn't worthy of the Hartleigh name.

When she reached the kitchen, Violet was talking into the telephone, apparently attempting to pacify whoever was on the other end. Judging from the housekeeper's repeated orders to calm down, the caller was in a high state of agitation.

With a strong sense of impending disaster, Elizabeth whispered urgently, "Who is it?"

"Winnie Pierce." Violet held out the receiver. "She sounds awful. Says she has to talk to you."

Beryl. Elizabeth placed the receiver against her ear and braced herself for bad news. "Winnie? Lady Elizabeth here. What's happened?"

She hardly recognized the agonized voice that answered her.

"It's Beryl, m'm," Winnie wailed. "They found her bicycle. Maude Dorsett's kids found it. Buried in the sand, it was. Down there on the beach below the coast road."

"Try to stay calm, Winnie, and take some deep breaths. The children didn't see Beryl?"

"No, m'm. No sign of her anywhere."

"Well, try not to worry. Just because her bicycle is there doesn't mean anything awful has happened to her. She could be anywhere. Have you called the hospital in North Horsham?"

"No, I haven't. I'm down here at the pub. I don't have a telephone at home. But George said he would call them."

Elizabeth raised her eyebrows. "You've talked to George Dalrymple?"

"I had to, m'm. See . . . the kids went straight to the police station. They found Beryl's handbag in the front basket. That's how they knew it was her bicycle." Winnie choked on a sob. "Something terrible has happened to my little girl, I just know it. She'd never go nowhere without her handbag. Not our Beryl wouldn't."

Elizabeth had to agree. This looked serious. Especially now that the police were involved. "I'll be right down. Put the kettle on, Winnie, and we'll have a nice cup of tea." She replaced the receiver and exchanged a worried glance with Violet. "Maude Dorsett's children found Beryl's bicycle," she explained.

"Beryl wasn't there?"

"No, but her handbag was in the basket. I must go down there and talk to poor Winnie. She's quite frantic."

Violet shook her head. "That child. Always causing trouble, she is. What do you think happened to her?"

"I don't know. But I don't like the implications." Elizabeth hurried out into the hallway and pulled her coat from the heavy oak hallstand. "I won't be long, Violet. Perhaps you should take down those curtains in the east wing while I'm gone. They should at least be cleaned. Martin will help you."

"Does he have to?"

"I think so." Elizabeth crammed her hat on her head and secured it with a large pin. "It does make him feel useful. Just put up with him for a bit, will you? There's a dear."

"All right, if I must. But you be careful, duck. I don't like the idea of you getting involved in police business. Doesn't look good for the lady of the manor to be involved with the police."

"It's not really police business yet, Violet, is it. After all, Beryl is only missing. She could be anywhere."

"Well, let's hope for the best." Violet uttered a heavy sigh. "I just wish the master was here, that I do. He knew how to take care of things."

Elizabeth swallowed her resentment. "You worry too much, Violet. I'm just going to talk to Winnie, that's all. Cheer her up a bit, I suppose. Anyway, I'll be back in time for supper."

"I certainly hope so."

Violet was still muttering something when Elizabeth ran lightly down the steps to the driveway. Her motorcycle was still parked where she'd left it earlier, and she climbed aboard, anxious now to be on her way. She'd tried to make light of things for Winnie's sake, but she was very much afraid that for once Beryl Pierce had met with more trouble than she could handle.

Winnie was waiting for her at the garden gate when Elizabeth roared down the lane. This time she managed to halt the motorcycle a little more gently and climbed off for once without tangling her skirt in the kick stand.

Leaving the machine parked close to the hedge, she followed Winnie up the garden path and did her best to understand the distracted woman's breathless comments.

"I just know she's in really bad trouble," Winnie moaned as she closed the door behind her guest. "George thinks she rode off the cliff in the dark and fell in the sea. But what would she be doing that far off the road, and how could she ride over the railing? It wasn't broken or nothing."

Standing in Winnie's cramped living room, Elizabeth did her best to sound optimistic. "Well, we don't want to jump to conclusions, do we. Was the bicycle damaged?"

"Front wheel buckled. Though George did say that could have happened with the sea throwing it up against the cliffs. I just wish Stan was here. He'd know what to do."

She led the way into her minuscule kitchen, where a kettle whistled loudly on the gas stove. Elizabeth shooed a fat, gray cat off one of the chairs and sat down. "Did George keep Beryl's handbag?"

"No, m'm. It's upstairs. He left it in Beryl's bedroom after he searched in there."

"Did he find anything significant?"

Violet poured a small amount of the steaming water into her teapot, swished it around, then emptied it in the sink. "Not really. He didn't look that close. You know George, always anxious to be somewhere else."

Elizabeth wondered how George could possibly do his job if he was always in a hurry. "What about her handbag? Nothing in there out of the ordinary?"

Violet measured two large teaspoons of tea leaves into the teapot, then poured the boiling water on top of them. "Well, as a matter of fact, I did find something. I looked in it myself after George left. I don't know if he searched it or not. I haven't mentioned anything to him. I wanted to ask Beryl about it first." Her face crumpled up, and she began to cry. "That's if I ever see her again."

Elizabeth got to her feet and patted the woman's trembling shoulder. "There, there. I'm sure Beryl is fine. Let's drink our tea, and you can tell me what you found."

"I'm sorry for talking on so, Lady Elizabeth. It's ever so nice of you to come down here, really it is." Winnie dragged a large white handkerchief out of the pocket of her apron and loudly blew her nose. "It's just that at times like this I really miss my Stan. This bloody war and all." She stuffed the hankie back in her pocket. "I'm all right now. Honest. Would you care for a piece of Dundee cake? I just made it this morning."

"Lovely!" Elizabeth sat down on her chair again and waited while Winnie poured the tea, then cut a large slice from the dark brown cake layered with almonds.

"Wherever did you get the nuts?" she exclaimed as Winnie sat the delicate cake plate in front of her. "I haven't seen almonds since the war began."

"Left over from Christmas." Winnie sat down on the other side of the small table and pulled her cup and saucer toward her. "Beryl got them for me, though she wouldn't say where. Black market, of course." She sent Elizabeth a guilty look. "Sorry, m'm, but everyone's doing it. Only way to survive, isn't it. None of us would have nothing if we didn't grab what we could when it's offered."

"That's all right, Winnie." Elizabeth bit into the soft, flavorful cake with relish. Although she wouldn't admit it, of course, she wasn't above bending the law herself now and then, if the occasion warranted it. After all, it was wartime. One did what one had to do. "This is really very good," she declared.

"Thank you, m'm. I do my best. That's a new recipe. Not bad, considering there are no eggs in there."

"There are no eggs? How marvelous!"

"I'll give you the recipe if you like."

"I'd love it. Violet hasn't made a cake since rationing began." She popped another piece in her mouth and savored every bite. "Now, tell me what you found in Beryl's handbag."

"Well, m'm, it was a train ticket. Here, I still got it in my pocket." Winnie fished in her pocket and came up with a small white card. "It's for London."

Elizabeth took the card and examined it. "It's a one-way ticket," she said in surprise.

"So I noticed," Winnie muttered. "That little bugger was planning on leaving and going up to London. Never said a word to me about it. She knew I would never let her go, of course. Not with all those bombs dropping all the time." She looked appealingly at Elizabeth. "Why would a young girl like her want to go to London, what with all those air raids and unexploded bombs and all? She must be crazy."

Elizabeth could think of a couple of reasons Beryl would prefer London to the sleepy existence of Sitting Marsh, but she refrained from mentioning them. "Well, obviously she's not there or she would have taken the ticket. What about her clothes?"

"All hanging in her wardrobe, same as usual."

"She hadn't packed anything?"

"Not even a handkerchief. Her suitcase is still lying on top of her wardrobe, and it's empty."

Elizabeth looked at the ticket again. "Then she wasn't planning on leaving right away. This ticket is valid for three months."

"You know what else is strange?" Winnie put her cup down in the saucer with a loud clatter. "I found something else in Beryl's handbag. It's an application to join the Land Army, from the recruitment center in North Horsham."

"Really?" Elizabeth raised her eyebrows. "I wouldn't have thought Beryl would be interested in working on the land. I thought she enjoyed her job at the canning factory."

"Oh, she does, m'm. And that's a fact." Winnie dug into her apron pocket and pulled out a crumpled pack of cigarettes. She offered them to Elizabeth, who declined with a shake of her head.

"Thank you, but that's one habit I never did acquire."

"Nor did I, m'm, until Stan left to fight the Germans. Helps put up with the loneliness, you see."

Certainly better than the way some women had cured loneliness, Elizabeth thought darkly. "You were saying that Beryl seems happy with her job."

"Oh, that's right. Yes, well, she's met lots of nice people there, she has. That's what surprised me about that Land Army thing. Our Beryl is not the type to muck about on a farm. She's just not strong enough to lift anything heavy, and she hates farm animals. Frightened of them, she is."

Frightened of hard work more likely, Elizabeth thought. "It does seem strange that she would consider joining the Land Army if she was planning on moving to London," she said slowly.

"Exactly what I thought." Winnie picked up her teacup and began swishing it around, then turned the cup upside down in her saucer. "Just wanted to see what my fortune was," she said, meeting Elizabeth's gaze. "You never know."

Elizabeth didn't really believe in all that nonsense, but she was intrigued nevertheless. She watched Winnie pick up her cup and peer cautiously at it.

"I'm getting a visitor," Winnie murmured. "Soon. Carrying a heart." She looked up. "Maybe it's my Stan getting a spot of leave."

"Let's hope so." Elizabeth smiled. "Anything else?"

"No, it's all cloudy at the bottom. Lots of confusion. Can't really tell anything from that. It happens sometimes." She set the cup down. "Like me to tell yours?"

"Oh, I don't know . . ." Elizabeth hesitated, then

handed over her cup. What harm could it do? Besides, it helped to keep Winnie's mind off her troubles for a while.

Winnie performed the same ritual with Elizabeth's cup, swishing it around three times, then turning it upside down on the saucer. After a moment or two she picked up the cup again and peered inside. "Oh, my," she exclaimed, her voice quickening. "You are going to have such a time. Lots of coming and going, lots of people all around you."

No doubt, Elizabeth thought grimly, with the invasion of the American air force in her home.

Winnie squinted her eyes. "What's this?" She peered closer. "You know a gentleman whose name begins with an *M*?"

"Martin," Elizabeth said promptly.

"I don't think so." Winnie lifted her face, and her eyes seemed to glisten with anticipation. "Whoever he is, m'm, it isn't Martin. That's for sure. This one's going to become very important to you, if you get my meaning. Very important, indeed."

CHAPTER

❀ 4 ❀

Elizabeth swallowed. "I don't think that's at all possible, Winnie, but thank you." She got to her feet and brushed a stray crumb from her skirt. "I wonder if you'd mind showing me Beryl's bedroom? I know George Dalrymple took a look at it, and I'm sure you have, too, but you might have missed something that would give us a clue to Beryl's whereabouts. Perhaps if we look together we might find something."

She'd made the suggestion more to change the subject than anything, but Winnie jumped to her feet at once. "That's a good idea, Lady Elizabeth. It's really good of you to offer to help. I'm ever so grateful. Really, I am."

"I'm not saying I can be of any real help," Elizabeth said, following Winnie up the narrow staircase.

"Just having something to do helps," Winnie assured her. "I feel so useless just sitting around waiting for her to come home." She opened the door to a tiny bedroom and stood back to allow Elizabeth to enter.

The room was charming, with a sloping roof that slanted down to where the blue lace-edged curtains at the window matched the eiderdown on the bed. There was just enough room to squeeze between the bed and the wardrobe on one side, while a small bedside table with a lamp fitted snugly against the wall on the other side. Beryl had pinned pictures of film stars above her bed, and Elizabeth recognized Clark Gable and Cary Grant among the collection.

Winnie showed her the empty suitcase and the crammed contents of the wardrobe. A row of shoes with platform soles sat beneath the dresses, skirts, and blouses. "Spends all her clothing coupons as soon as she gets them," Winnie murmured.

Most of her mother's, too, Elizabeth thought, eyeing the well-stocked wardrobe. "Nothing in the pockets?" she asked.

Winnie shook her head. "George had me go through them all."

Elizabeth turned her attention back to the bed. "You know," she said softly, "when I was a young girl and wanted to keep something important safe, I always tucked it inside my pillow." She reached under the eiderdown and drew out a large, fluffy pillow. "May I?"

"Certainly, m'm."

Elizabeth slipped her hand inside the pillow case, then caught her breath when her searching fingers encountered something. She withdrew a small white envelope.

"Well, I'll be blowed. Would you look at that!" Winnie said in a hushed voice.

Elizabeth offered her the letter.

"You open it, m'm, if you would. I don't have my glasses up here."

Carefully Elizabeth withdrew the folded sheet of paper and opened it. "It's a love letter," she said after quickly scanning the lines, "from someone called Robbie."

Winnie frowned and held out her hand for the letter. "May I, m'm?" She squinted at it for a second or two, then raised her head. "I don't know what our Beryl's been up to," she said slowly, "but I've never heard of no one called Robbie in my life."

"Well, obviously Beryl knows him. Judging from the sentiments scribbled on this note, I'd say they know each other very well." Elizabeth met Winnie's anxious gaze. "Would you mind if I have a look in the wardrobe?"

"No, not at all." Winnie sank onto the end of the bed. "I just don't know what's come over our Beryl, really I don't. She never used to be like this when Stan was home. She's been acting really strange lately. You know what she did last Saturday morning? She had all her hair cut off, that's what. All that beautiful thick hair. Looked like a boy, she did. I told her how terrible it looked. That was the last day I saw her—" Winnie's voice cracked, and she buried her face in the folds of her apron. "Sorry, m'm."

Elizabeth's heart ached at the pain in that muffled voice. No matter what, she would find out what had happened to Beryl if she had to turn the entire countryside upside down to do it.

She turned her attention to the wardrobe, running her hands through the clothes, though she didn't really know what she was looking for. Winnie had already searched the pockets, and there didn't seem to be anything on the floor except for the shoes.

She was about to close the door when something bright and shiny caught her eye. She moved a dark blue woolen dress aside and took down a black blazer, adorned with bold, brass buttons. It wasn't the brass that had glinted at her from the darkness of the wardrobe, however, it was a small enameled badge pinned to one of the lapels.

Elizabeth took a closer look. "Your husband is in the navy, isn't he?"

"Stan? Yes, he volunteered last year. Always loved the sea, he did."

"Do you have any members of your family serving in the Royal Engineers?"

Winnie looked puzzled. "No, m'm, not as I know of. My brother's in the infantry, and a cousin's in the Royal Artillery. The rest are in the air force, those who are called up, anyway."

"Then this could belong to Beryl's friend Robbie." Elizabeth showed her the jacket with the regimental badge pinned to it.

"Oh, my." Winnie took the jacket in her hands and stared at the pin. "What will Evan say to this? He'll be really upset if he finds out Beryl's been keeping company with a soldier." She looked up, a worried frown creasing her forehead. "You know, ever since the army turned him down, he's had it in for soldiers. Turned him bitter, it did. He wanted to join up so bad and get away from that farm. Flat feet, they said. He wouldn't be able to march."

"Well, I'm sure he's needed just as much on the farm," Elizabeth said, closing the door of the wardrobe. "There are so few men left to take care of the land now. If it wasn't for the women in the Land Army, there would be no farms for the men to come back to after the war."

"Don't I know it." Winnie sighed. "Do you think that Beryl might be with this Robbie person?"

"I think it's a possibility. Would you mind if I take the badge with me? Perhaps I'll be able to find out who this man is, and he might at least know where Beryl has

gone. I'd also like to take the train ticket, the letter, and
the Land Army application. I really don't know what help
they would be, but I'd like to take a closer look at everything."

"Oh, thank you, Lady Elizabeth." Winnie rose slowly
to her feet. "I don't know which way to turn anymore. I
just want my little girl to come back home, that's all."

"I know," Elizabeth said gently. "And I'm going to do
everything I can to see that that happens."

She left a few minutes later, having refused Winnie's
offer of another cup of tea. It was beginning to get dark,
and Evan would be coming back home from the fields
about now. She was anxious to have a word with that
young man.

Evan's mother welcomed her unexpected visitor with
flustered concern and effusive apologies for the state of
the house. Daphne Potter was a better-than-average
housewife and kept the ancient farmhouse spotless, but
like most of the residents of Sitting Marsh, a visit from
the lady of the manor warranted a thorough spring cleaning, and she was dismayed at the lack of opportunity to
prepare her home for such an illustrious occasion.

She ushered her guest into the front parlor, which was
kept solely for the use of visitors. In spite of the summer
warmth outside, the damp cushions of the sofa Elizabeth
sat upon were a clear indication that the Potters hadn't
had any visitors in some time. The room smelled faintly
of apple cider, wet wool, and stale cigars. Elizabeth declined to take off her coat. Even the mansion, with it's
drafty windows and lack of appreciable heating in the
winter, didn't feel as chillingly moist as this room.

"I suppose you've come to talk to Evan," Daphne Potter said when Elizabeth refused her offer of tea. "He'll
be in any minute. He was talking to George for a while,

so that put him behind a bit. Such a shame about Beryl.
I wonder where she can be. Our Evan is near out of his
mind with worry, poor lamb. Thinks the world of her, he
does."

"Yes, well, they've been going out together for some
time," Elizabeth murmured. "I don't suppose Evan has
any ideas where she might be?"

"None at all. Complete mystery to him. He were that
upset when he came home Saturday night. I heard him
slam the door really hard, the way he always does when
he and Beryl have been fighting. I thought they'd had
another row."

"What time was that?" Elizabeth asked, trying to sound
casual about it. "When he came home Saturday, I mean."

"Oh, must have been after eleven. Jim had just come
to bed. He always stays up to listen to the latest news.
Don't know why. It's all so depressing, isn't it. Though
I must say, Mr. Churchill has some good things to say.
Makes one really proud to be British, that's what I say."

"Did Evan say anything when he came in on Saturday
night?"

Daphne Potter looked surprised. "Not a word. I didn't
know until the next day that Beryl never turned up to
meet him. Spent all day moping around the house, he
did. Went and helped his dad in the fields that afternoon.
He never does that as a rule. Could have knocked Jim
down with a feather."

She turned sharply as a door slammed somewhere deep
in the house. "That'll be Evan and our Jim back now. If
you'll excuse me, Lady Elizabeth, I'll go and tell them
you're here. I expect Evan will want to clean up a bit
before he talks to you."

"Oh, that really isn't necessary," Elizabeth said, knowing full well her protest would be ignored.

"He won't be long. Are you sure I can't get you a nice cup of tea?"

Elizabeth would have preferred something a little stronger, but since good sherry and spirits were almost impossible to get nowadays, she reluctantly accepted Daphne Potter's offer. "Thank you, that would be lovely." At least it would warm her up a little.

Evan arrived at the parlor just as she was finishing the strong brew. He hovered in the doorway, looking as if he were ready to bolt at any given moment. "Mum said you wanted to see me, Lady Elizabeth?"

She smiled and waved a hand at the faded armchair sitting in the corner of the room. "Come in, Evan. I wanted to say how sorry I am about this dreadful business with Beryl."

"Yes, m'm." Evan perched his backside gingerly on the edge of the chair and thrust his hands between his knees. He was a sturdy young man with the ruddy cheeks and strong shoulders of the true farmer. Seeing him right then, looking so hale and hearty, it was hard to imagine that he'd been denied the opportunity to fight alongside his fellow farmers for his country.

"Tell me what happened between you and Beryl," Elizabeth began. "Did you have any kind of an argument the last time you saw her?"

Evan looked surprised, and she added hurriedly, "I know this is none of my business, but I promised her mother I'd see what I could do to find her, so anything you can tell me that might help would be greatly appreciated."

"I don't know as how I can help at all," Evan said, his cheeks turning a dark crimson. "I already talked to George and told him everything I know, which ain't much."

"I know, but maybe there's something you might have missed. Besides, I always find that talking about troubles sometimes lightens the load." She wondered if Evan knew about Robbie, but she hesitated to ask. The poor boy must be in enough agony wondering what happened to his girlfriend, without aggravating him with more bad news.

"All I know is, she didn't turn up for our date. We were supposed to meet at seven o'clock that Saturday night, outside the Tudor Arms. I hadn't seen her in two days, and I was really looking forward to being with her. Well, I waited until eight o'clock that night, and she didn't come. I was really fed up about it, so I went in the pub on my own to have a drink."

"And you were there the rest of the evening?"

"Until closing time, yeah. Then I came home. I went straight to bed and I didn't go out again until I went into the fields with me dad on Monday morning. I told George all this already. He told me some kids found her bicycle on the beach. I don't know what happened to her. Maybe she's run off with someone. Wouldn't put it past her."

On an impulse, Elizabeth asked carefully, "Evan, do you know a soldier by the name of Robbie? He's in the Royal Engineers, I believe."

Evan's dark brown eyes met hers without a waver. "Never heard of him. What's he got to do with anything?"

"I don't know. Maybe nothing." She took a deep breath. "But Beryl apparently knows someone of that name, and she was wearing a regimental badge on the lapel of her jacket."

Evan gave his head a slight shake, as if he didn't really believe what she was saying. "I don't know nothing about that. All I know is that she was supposed to meet me, and she didn't turn up. What happened to her after that, I've got no idea."

"Well, thank you, Evan." Elizabeth rose to her feet. "I appreciate you taking the time to talk to me."

Now that the inquisition was apparently over, Evan seemed to spring to life. He jumped to his feet and rushed to open the door for her. "Thank you for coming, Lady Elizabeth. If there's anything I can do to help, you only have to ask. All right?"

Elizabeth smiled. "I might just do that, Evan. Thank you. I sincerely hope that this matter can be cleared up very quickly, and Beryl will return to her home. I'm sure she must know how worried everyone is about her."

"Beryl doesn't always think like that, does she. She can be really selfish at times."

"Well, I hope that's all it is. Please say good night to your parents for me." She left hurriedly, eager to be on her way. There was one more stop she wanted to make— the Tudor Arms—and she wanted to be there before it got too busy.

The car park was empty when she pulled up outside the pub. In the gathering darkness the heavy black beams that crisscrossed the white walls looked even more imposing. Lights blazed from the lattice windows, spilling across a row of bicycles propped against the fence.

The acrid odor of cigarette smoke and beer threatened to suffocate her when she entered the warmth of the hazy lounge bar. Above her head various brass pots, pans, and kettles dangled from the heavy beams that supported the low ceiling and threatened anyone with more than an average height a mighty good clonk on the head.

Two men stood at the long, burn-scarred counter. They looked up as she approached, the younger of the two giving a start of surprise when he apparently recognized her. In the corner by the fireplace, two more men sat deep in quiet conversation.

Alfie, the bartender, hurried forward with a look of astonishment on his round, flushed face. "Lady Elizabeth! What a surprise to see you here. What would you like, then?" He took a hurried swipe at the counter with a grubby-looking cloth.

"A sherry, please, if you have one," Elizabeth said promptly. As long as she was here, she might as well enjoy one of life's simple pleasures.

"Sorry, m'm. No sherry this month. Got a nice drop of port, though. Will that do?"

"That will do very nicely, thank you." Elizabeth smiled at the two customers, both of whom were staring at her in undisguised curiosity. She realized that it probably wasn't terribly appropriate for her to be in a public house unescorted. But then, this was wartime, and nothing was quite the same as it once was. One must become accustomed to all sorts of things these days.

Recognizing Jack Mitchem, the local butcher, she nodded affably. "Good evening, Mr. Mitchem. I haven't seen you in quite a while. I do hope the business is going well, all things considered?"

"Very well, m'm, thank you." As if suddenly remembering his manners, he added, "May I introduce you to my father, Tom Mitchem? Came down from the Smoke for a while, he has. Getting a little too noisy for him up there. Pop, this is Lady Elizabeth Hartleigh, from the Manor House."

Elizabeth gave the elderly man a sympathetic smile. "I imagine living in London these days must be quite traumatic. How nice that you can get a respite for a while in our quiet little village."

The butcher's father looked as if he didn't understand

a word she'd said, but he nodded and smiled anyway.

Alfie returned to the counter and set down a small glass half filled with the dark red liquid. Elizabeth opened her handbag, but Alfie held up his hands. "On the house, Lady Elizabeth. After all, it isn't every day we get a visit from the lady of the manor."

"That's very kind of you, Alfred. Thank you." Elizabeth took a dainty sip from the glass and discreetly swished the potent wine around her tongue before swallowing it. "Now, I wonder if I could have a word with you?" She glanced at the two men at her side. "It's rather private."

Jack Mitchem lifted two foaming glasses of beer off the counter. "Well, if you'll excuse us, m'm, we'll find ourselves a table."

Elizabeth waited until the two men had settled themselves across the room before turning back to Alfie. "I suppose you have heard about Beryl Pierce disappearing?"

Alfie nodded. "Nasty business. I heard they found her bike down on the beach. Drowned in the sea, I expect, poor little bugger."

"Oh, dear, I do hope not." Though she had to admit the possibility seemed logical. "I was wondering, Alfred, if you happened to notice Evan Potter here in the lounge on Saturday night."

"Yes, m'm, I saw him. Sat all by himself in that corner, he did." Alfie nodded to a corner of the room by the narrow windows. "Didn't want to talk to no one that night. Can't say as I blame him, seeing as how his girlfriend didn't turn up."

"Did you happen to notice what time he left?"

Alfie shook his head. "Gets real busy around about closing time. Those Yanks never want to leave. I can yell,

'Time, gentlemen, please,' over and over again, as loud as I like. They don't take no notice. I have to practically shove them out the door. I think Evan left about the same time as everyone else, though."

Elizabeth nodded. "Well, thank you, Alfred."

Alfie looked worried. "Here, he's not in any trouble, is he? I mean, I wouldn't want to get him in any bother, or nothing like that. I didn't see him leave, but—"

"Don't worry, Alfred." Elizabeth drained the last of the port and set down her glass. "I was just curious, that's all. No harm done."

Just then the street door swung open, and a group of Americans entered, all seemingly talking at once.

Elizabeth picked up her handbag, nodded at Alfie, then quickly crossed the room.

One of the American airmen, a freckle-faced youth who looked as if he hadn't eaten a proper meal in months, stepped in front of her as she reached the door.

"Hey, there, gorgeous," he drawled in his distinctive accent. "How about keeping a lonesome flier company for a while? I reckon a cute chick like you knows how to have some fun, right?"

Elizabeth reminded herself how far these young men were from home and how imperative it was to remain on good terms with England's American allies. "Thank you," she said firmly, "but I make it a policy never to date anyone until we've been properly introduced and I've been acquainted with him for at least six months."

While the American was still struggling to digest that, she slipped past him and out into the cool, clean sea air. Roaring up the High Street on her motorcycle, she wondered how many times Beryl had been approached by one of those brash Americans. There were just too many temptations for a young, impressionable girl of Beryl's tender age, and too many opportunities for getting into trouble.

Whatever trouble Beryl Pierce was in, however, Elizabeth was painfully aware that she was no closer to the answers. As time went on with no word from the child, it seemed likely that she'd met with some kind of accident. If she had drowned in the sea, as the bartender had suggested, her mother would be absolutely devastated. Elizabeth ached for the poor woman. So many people were dying these days in this dreadful war. To perish so young from something as preventable as a simple accident would be such a terrible, senseless waste.

Elizabeth bent her head against the buffeting wind and hoped with all her heart that her fears were unfounded. Somehow she had to find out the truth. It would seem that she had taken on a formidable task, but she couldn't give up now. Someone, somewhere, must know what had happened that fateful morning, when a young girl left her home and never came back. That person could well be the mysterious Robbie. Somehow she had to find him. And soon.

CHAPTER

❈ 5 ❈

"I hope you're holding this thing steady," Violet muttered as she mounted the steps of the ladder. "I should have made you go up here instead of me."

"As you very well know, Violet, I have absolutely no head for heights." Martin's voice was muffled by the necessity of holding his chin firmly pressed to his chest in order to avoid looking up Violet's skirts.

"Well, neither do I, but sometimes we all have to do what we don't like to do." Violet reached up and tugged at the hooks fastened securely to the curtain rod. "These things are rusted. No wonder I can't get them to blinking move. I should have waited for Polly to help me."

"I always find that when something refuses to budge, a good pounding with a hammer often does the trick."

"Remind me of that the next time you take half an hour to get up from the breakfast table." Violet groaned and tugged harder. "I don't know why we have to wash these things, anyhow. They're bound to fall apart as soon as I put them in the water. If you ask me, the Yanks will never notice if the curtains are washed or not."

"Yanks? Who is Yanks? Madam didn't tell me we were having a house guest."

"We're having more than one guest, Martin. We're having a whole crowd of them. We'll be having Americans crawling all over this house by next week."

Martin uttered a shocked cry. "When did you find out about this? Does madam know?"

"Of course she blinking knows." Violet hung onto the curtains and pulled with all her might.

"Why didn't she tell me? What are we going to do? Good Lord, woman, we're being invaded. Where are the police? Where is the army? I demand they protect us."

Doing her best to ignore Martin's ranting, Violet jerked hard on the curtains. "We're not being invaded, Martin, we—" She broke off with sharp exclamation as the curtains finally let go their death grip on the rod and parted company. Deprived of her secure hold, Violet lost her balance and had to let go of the heavy fabric to steady herself.

The curtains descended, en masse, and draped themselves lovingly on top of Martin. With an agonized scream, he started flailing wildly in a frantic attempt to escape.

"Stand still, you daft sod!" Violet yelled. "You'll have me off here." She began scrambling down the ladder, just as Martin blindly stumbled into it. The ladder rocked and then in slow motion toppled over and crashed to the ground.

Luckily for Violet, she landed on top of Martin, who momentarily stopped struggling. For one terrible moment she thought she might have killed him. She scrambled to her feet and started tugging at the suffocating folds to free him.

"You'll never take me alive!" Martin shouted, thus immensely relieving Violet, who was already rehearsing how she'd tell Lizzie that Martin had permanently departed.

"Stand still, you old fool!" she yelled. "It's only me."

Martin, however, continued to yell and struggle, and by the time she finally got him out of his cocoon, she was exhausted.

Released from bondage, Martin stared wildly around the room. "By Jove, that was a close call." He struggled to his knees, then made a supreme effort to get back on his feet. "We have to find madam and warn her the invasion has begun."

"It's not an invasion," Violet began, but Martin didn't wait to hear the rest of her sentence.

"Come on, Violet, we have to find a place to hide before they come back." He shuffled out of the door, shouting, "Head for the hills! The invasion has begun!"

Violet closed her eyes. All this and a houseful of Yanks, too. It just didn't bear thinking about.

"I'm so glad you're home," Violet told Elizabeth. "Where have you been? I expected you ages ago."

Elizabeth peered past her into the dark shadows of the entrance hall. "Martin taking a nap?"

"Not exactly." Violet leaned against the heavy door to close it. "He's sipping on a brandy in the kitchen at the moment."

"I didn't know we had any brandy," Elizabeth said, starting for the kitchen stairs.

"One bottle. I keep it for medicinal purposes."

"What's the matter with Martin, then?"

"He found out about the Yanks coming to stay here."

Elizabeth paused halfway down the stairs. "Oh, no. How did that happen?"

"I told him, didn't I. I thought you'd already talked to him about it."

"No, I was waiting for the right time." Elizabeth glanced guiltily at the kitchen door. "I was worried it might upset him."

"Yes, you could say that. He thinks we're being invaded. I keep telling him that Yanks are not the same as the Germans, but I don't think he understands."

Elizabeth sighed and continued on down the steps. "Perhaps I should have a word with him. I might be able to calm him down."

"I bloomin' hope so. He's been carrying on something awful."

Elizabeth pushed open the kitchen door and peered in.

Martin sat at the table, his face buried in his trembling hands. He didn't even look up when she spoke his name.

Elizabeth advanced into the room and gently laid a hand on his shoulder. "Martin? Are you all right?"

"It's the end of the world as we know it," he said, his voice muffled in his palms.

"Nonsense," Elizabeth said briskly. "We're having a few house guests for a while, that's all. Nothing to be alarmed about."

Slowly he dropped his hands and peered at her over the top of his glasses. "Madam? What are you doing here?" Before she could stop him, he'd stumbled to his feet. "We must find a place to hide. This is a ghastly war. The enemy have totally surrounded the house. They tried to suffocate me. They're arriving in those infernal flying machines and are landing everywhere. Those savages can lop off your head with one blow of their swords."

"American airmen don't carry swords, Martin. You're getting them confused with someone else. I don't want you to worry about this. Violet and I can take care of everything—"

"They're just a bunch of blinking cowboys," Violet put in from the doorway.

"Cowboys?" Martin sank onto his chair again. "No, no, madam, we can't have cowboys here. We don't have enough room in the stables. There'll be horses all over the lawn. The gardener will never be able to cope. And what if they bring wild Indians with them? Dreadful savages, madam. They'll cut off all our hair."

"They'd have to find yours first," Violet said dryly. She stood just inside the door, her arms folded, her head to one side. "Barmy as a dim-witted goat, he is. I told you he'd go off the edge one day."

"He's just confused," Elizabeth said, sending Violet a warning frown. She patted Martin's shoulder. "Listen to me, Martin. Nothing bad is going to happen to any of us. There are no Germans and no enemy. Some very nice American officers are coming to stay with us for a while, that's all. I think it might be rather fun, don't you?"

"Oh, it'll be fun, all right," Violet muttered. "About as much fun as a blinking picnic in a field of angry bulls."

"Bulls? Where?" Martin demanded. "Where are they? I'll need my shotgun."

"You haven't touched a shotgun in fifty years, you silly old goat." Violet marched toward him. "Now what have I been trying to tell you? Madam has invited these gentlemen here, and she wouldn't invite savages to the house, now would she?" She sent Elizabeth a sly look. "Besides, I wouldn't be at all surprised if we don't do very well out of them Yanks. From what I hear, they can get just about everything on that base of theirs. Things like cigarettes and chocolates and nylon stockings—"

"Violet!" Martin looked scandalized. "Not in front of madam."

"And sherry and Scotch . . ."

Martin's eyes brightened visibly. "Scotch?"

"Violet, I don't think—" Elizabeth began.

"Scotch," Violet said firmly. She threw her arms open wide. "Whole big bottles of it. As many as you want."

"Violet, perhaps we shouldn't—"

"Bottles of Scotch?" Martin straightened, the magic words apparently restoring sanity. "Well, I suppose it wouldn't hurt to have a few cowboys around the house. As long as we keep a strict eye on them, of course, what? Can't have them rounding up John Miller's cows, now can we?"

"I don't think we should encourage him," Elizabeth murmured. "I rather imagine it's illegal for the Americans to give us any of their supplies."

"I'm sure," Violet said cheerfully. "But no one seems to mind, do they."

"Which doesn't exactly make it right."

"No worse than pinching a few extra bottles of orange juice for Betty Brown's baby, I'd say."

Elizabeth lifted her chin. "That was an emergency. The child was sick."

Violet nodded. "Tell that to the authorities."

She had no good answer to that. Instead, Elizabeth turned back to her aging butler. "Perhaps you should go to your room now, Martin, and take a nice nap. Violet will be along shortly with your dinner."

"Such as it is." Violet hurried over to the stove, where a large pot bubbled on the gas ring. "It's impossible to make a good stew these days, with what little meat they allow us on ration. I have to doctor it up with all sorts of stuff to give it any kind of taste."

Which probably accounted for the strange odor, Elizabeth thought sourly. She dreaded to think what Violet had thrown into that pot. She was even more afraid to ask. What one didn't know these days, the better off one was.

It was much later that night when she woke up suddenly out of a bad dream. No doubt Violet's obnoxious stew, she thought as she lay staring at the dark ceiling. The concoction had been even worse than she'd anticipated. There had to be recipes out there somewhere that would make even wartime rations at least palatable. She would have to hunt some down somewhere. Maybe Winnie Pierce could help.

Thinking of Winnie gave her a pang of anxiety. She'd promised to help find Beryl, and so far she'd been no help at all. She reached out and fumbled with the switch on her bedside lamp, flooding the room with soft light.

Her handbag lay on her comfortable wicker armchair, and she emptied the contents onto her bed. A train ticket to London, a love letter, a regimental badge, and a form from the Land Army. The application hadn't been filled in. Obviously Beryl hadn't found the time or the enthusiasm to do so yet.

Staring at the assortment of objects on her pink-flowered eiderdown, Elizabeth had to admit they didn't add up to a lot. There wasn't anything there that could give her any answers. There had to be some way of finding this Robbie person.

Not that Elizabeth expected Beryl to be with him, even if she did find him. Why would Beryl leave everything behind, and her bicycle on the beach, to go off with someone she hardly knew? On the other hand, if she had fallen over the cliffs into the sea, she would have had to plow through a tangle of barbed wire first.

The more Elizabeth thought about it, the more likely it seemed that Beryl either jumped over that cliff or was thrown from it. And while she was about it, she'd take a look at that bicycle.

A light rain sprinkled the vast lawns as she ran down the steps the next morning. The sweet fragrance of roses hung heavy in the air, and she paused to enjoy the aroma before marching to what used to be the stables, her feet in their sensible shoes crunching on the gravel.

She was dragging her motorcycle out from one of the empty stalls when Desmond, the gardener, appeared at her side. He stood twisting his cap in his hands, and his bushy white eyebrows twitched up and down in agitation.

Desmond was too old to be inducted into the army. It was Elizabeth's considered opinion that he was also too old to take care of grounds as vast as those surrounding the Manor House, but somehow he managed. She'd hired him when her regular gardener had been called up. Desmond had pleaded with her for the job, saying he'd go "starkers" if he didn't have something to do. He'd been employed as a paperhanger before the war, but no one was papering their walls anymore. Not with a war on.

Elizabeth peered at his corrugated face with some concern. "Is something wrong, Desmond?"

"Well, m'm, I don't rightly know. It were Martin what told me, and you know how Martin is. I never know if he's telling the truth or if it's all in his head, if you get my meaning."

Elizabeth knew only too well what he meant. "What did Martin tell you, then?"

"He said as how there were going to be cowboys and Indians running around here, m'm."

"Martin was mistaken, Desmond."

"Yes, m'm. I didn't think so. I mean, it would have been all right. I would have had to clean out the stables, though, for the horses and—"

"Desmond," Elizabeth said gently.

"Yes, m'm?"

"No cowboys and Indians."

"Right, m'm."

"Though we will have some American officers staying with us for a while. They shouldn't affect you, though."

"No, m'm. What about vehicles, though?"

"Vehicles?"

"Yes, m'm. Army vehicles. Don't the Americans drive them jeeps?"

"Oh, Lord, I'd forgotten about that." Elizabeth cast an anxious glance around the courtyard. "I suppose they could use this as a car park. I'll have to have a word with Major Monroe about it." Winnie's voice seemed to repeat softly in her ear. *"A gentleman whose name begins with an M."* Annoyed with herself, she said hurriedly, "I'll let you know as soon as I can, Desmond."

"Yes, m'm." Desmond touched his forehead with his fingers, then shuffled around the corner out of sight.

Determined to put her worries about the Americans out of her mind for the time being, Elizabeth took off at a smart pace and a few minutes later arrived at the Pierce cottage. The door opened the moment she knocked, and she felt awful when she saw the hope on Winnie's face.

"I'm sorry," she said quickly, "no more news, I'm afraid. I would like to come in, though, if you have a minute?"

"Oh, of course, Lady Elizabeth. You're welcome any-time." Winnie managed to hide her disappointment quite well as she led Elizabeth into the parlor. "I've just made some tea. Can I get you a cup?"

"Thank you, but I just finished breakfast a short time ago." Elizabeth dropped her handbag on the sofa. "I was wondering if the police brought back Beryl's bicycle."

"Yes, m'm, George walked it up the hill. Can't ride it, of course, until I get the wheel mended. It's outside in the garden."

Elizabeth followed her out of the back door where a tangled mass of white daisies and marigolds lined a pebble path that led to a tool shed at the bottom of the garden. An aging apple tree spread gnarled and twisted branches over a small lawn, where plaster elves lurked around a stone birdbath.

Elizabeth, as always, was enchanted by the delightful confusion of the typical English garden. Sometimes the pristine flower beds and smooth lawns of the mansion irked her, mocking her with their smug perfection in a chaotic world. It seemed wrong, somehow, to spend so much time weeding and pruning flower beds, when elsewhere homes and everything in them were being blown to smithereens.

The front wheel of Beryl's bicycle was badly mangled, though the basket had remained intact. As George Dalrymple had observed, it was possible the damage had been done by the force of the sea. Though judging by the dents in the frame, the fall from the cliff seemed more likely.

The small leather pouch behind the saddle was still intact. Elizabeth studied it for a moment. "Was there anything in the saddlebag?"

"I don't know," Winnie said, sounding a little agitated. "I never gave it a thought. I don't know if George looked in there. He never said—" She broke off as Elizabeth undid the flaps and drew out a thickly folded sheet of paper. "Whatever's that?"

"It's a map." Elizabeth unfolded the large piece of paper and studied it. "Oh, isn't this interesting. It's a map of America."

"What?" Winnie peered over her shoulder. "Why, that little cow. I strictly forbade her to go anywhere near that American base."

"Well, I don't know if she went to the base or not," Elizabeth said, turning the map over to look at the back of it. "One thing I do know. This map came from there. Look, it has the price in cents."

"You think someone gave it to her?" Winnie's eyes widened. "An American? Don't tell me our Beryl has run off with a bloody Yank."

If she did, Elizabeth thought unhappily, *she went without her clothes and her handbag. And the love letter she'd tucked so carefully inside her pillow.* Much as she hated to admit it, she had a nasty feeling that Beryl hadn't run anywhere.

She stared at the map, thinking about that letter. Could Robbie be an American? If so, where did the regimental badge on Beryl's blazer come from? That most certainly belonged to a British soldier.

"I don't know what our Stan will say if Beryl's gone off with a Yank," Winnie muttered. "How am I going to tell him that? He'll have a fit."

Sensing that Winnie was clinging to that faint hope rather than contemplate the fact that Beryl might not be alive, Elizabeth made no comment. "I really should be running along," she said instead. "Would you mind if I take the map with me?" Not that she really expected it to be any more help than the rest of Beryl's belongings, but it seemed prudent to add it to the collection.

Winnie accompanied her on the path around the cottage to the front gate. "Are you sure you won't stop for a cup of tea?" she asked as she unhooked the latch. "I don't feel right sending you off without anything."

Elizabeth was about to reassure her when she saw the sturdy figure of Police Constable George Dalrymple, wearing his official helmet, winding his way on his bicycle around the bend in the lane. A sense of foreboding made her go cold. Maybe he was coming to give Winnie good news, she told herself, though now that she could see his grim expression, somehow she didn't think so.

Her own face must have given away her thoughts. Winnie turned sharply and clutched the collar of her cotton dress when she saw the constable wavering toward them. "Oh, please, God, no," she whispered.

George braked and steadied himself with a foot braced either side. After what seemed an eternity, he swung his leg awkwardly over the back of the saddle. With slow, deliberate movements that seemed to jar every nerve in Elizabeth's body, he leaned the bicycle against the hedge.

Winnie, apparently forgetting who she was with, clutched Elizabeth's arm with a painful grip. She stared at the constable, her pinched lips moving, though not a sound emerged from them.

George tipped his helmet at Elizabeth, then pulled a notepad from his breast pocket. For a moment it seemed as if the entire world were holding its breath. Not a whisper of a breeze sang among the branches of the ancient oak in front of the house. Even the birds appeared to have ceased chirping.

George loudly cleared his throat, then started to intone the dreaded words Elizabeth had been more or less expecting to hear ever since that battered bicycle had been found on the beach.

"Mrs. Pierce, I'm sorry to inform you that the body of your daughter, Beryl Anne Pierce—"

Elizabeth's heart sank. Her worst fears had been realized.

CHAPTER

6

George paused as a wretched cry tore from Winnie's lips. When he continued, his voice betrayed his deep sorrow.

"Beryl Pierce was discovered on the beach early this morning. She was deceased and presumed to have drowned. Please accept my sincere condolences."

Winnie's knees buckled, and Elizabeth caught hold of the distraught woman's arm. "Help me, George. Let's get her in the house."

George made a clumsy grab at Winnie's other arm, and between them they half carried her into the parlor, where she fell onto the sofa and gave herself up to deep, heart-wrenching sobs.

"Brandy," Elizabeth said briskly. "That's what she needs. Look in the cupboards, George, and see if you can find some."

"Haven't seen brandy in months," George muttered,

but he ambled obediently into the kitchen and began opening and shutting cupboards.

Winnie rocked to and fro on the sofa, unheeding of Elizabeth's attempts to calm her. "What am I going to do?" she wailed. "She was my only one and now she's gone."

There were no words in Elizabeth's mind that could possibly comfort the poor woman right then. All she could do was pat a shuddering shoulder and repeat over and over again, "I'm sorry, Winnie. I'm so dreadfully sorry."

George came back carrying a bottle half filled with golden liquid. "Seems like everyone has brandy in the house except me," he grumbled.

"That's because everyone keeps it for medicinal purposes and doesn't consume it the moment they get their hands on it," Elizabeth said tartly. "Did you bring a glass?"

George plodded back to the kitchen and returned a moment later with a beer mug. "All I could find."

"It will have to do." Elizabeth poured a small measure of the brandy into the mug and held it to Winnie's lips. "Here, Winnie, drink this."

Winnie shook her head, still rocking back and forth, though her sobs seemed a little quieter.

"I should be getting along," George said, edging toward the door. "They'll be needing me down at the station. The medical examiner will be arriving shortly—"

Elizabeth cut him off before he could say anything that would further upset the weeping woman. "That's all right, George. I can manage from here. I assume Lieutenant Pierce will be informed?"

"Yes, m'm. It's already been taken care of."

"Thank you, George." She offered the mug to Winnie again. "Please drink this, my dear. It will make you feel a little calmer."

This time Winnie obediently sipped the burning liquid, shuddering as she swallowed.

George hesitated a moment longer, then let himself quietly out of the house.

Alone with the grieving mother, Elizabeth did her best to think of something to say that wouldn't sound trite.

"She didn't fall off that cliff," Winnie said distinctly.

"Now, now, try not to dwell too much on it," Elizabeth said uneasily. "I think we should wait until the doctor's report before we start making accusations. After all, we don't really know what happened yet, do we?"

"Nor are we likely to, not with those blinking fools in charge of the investigation. George and Sid will just put it down to an accident and forget about it. Neither one of them wants to be bothered with police work. You know that, m'm, just as well as I do."

Elizabeth was inclined to agree, but she refrained from saying so. "I'm sure they'll do their best, Winnie."

"It won't be good enough." Winnie reached out for Elizabeth's hand and clutched it tightly. "My Beryl has been riding back and forth along that road since she was six years old. She knew it as well as she knew her own hand. She wouldn't have gone anywhere near that barbed wire. One of her friends got cut on it once, and the bleeding wouldn't stop for hours. She was afraid of it."

As if suddenly realizing whom she was grasping, Winnie hastily let go of Elizabeth's hand. "Please, Lady Elizabeth, I know it's a lot to ask, but I don't have anyone else to turn to. Please find out what happened to my little girl. If someone did this to her, I want him found and punished. I shan't rest easy until I know what happened."

Neither would she now, Elizabeth thought grimly. "I don't know how much help I can be, Winnie, but I'll do my very best to find out what happened. That's all I can promise."

Winnie's face puckered again. "Thank you, m'm. I'm much obliged. And so will my Stan be, when he hears." Her voice wavered off into another bout of weeping, and it took Elizabeth several minutes and another good measure of brandy before she felt comfortable enough to leave the poor woman alone with her grief.

Upon her return to the mansion, she had to wait several minutes before Martin managed to get the door open. "Sorry, madam," he wheezed. "I had to find my glasses before I answered the bell."

Elizabeth didn't have the heart to tell him that until he learned to look through them, the absence of his glasses was no appreciable impediment. "That's all right, Martin. Has Polly arrived yet?"

"Yes, madam. I do believe she's in the dining room with Violet."

Elizabeth stepped into the cool fragrance of the entrance hall. "Has anyone rung today?" She'd rather expected Major Monroe to have called by now, letting her know exactly when he planned to move in his men.

"Rung, madam?" Martin looked confused.

She waited until he had struggled to close the door before explaining. "The telephone, Martin. Did anyone ring with a message?"

Martin tucked a finger under his nose and dug in his pocket. His sneeze exploded about the same time he dragged a handkerchief from his pocket. After several moments of fumbling, he managed to blow his nose and return the handkerchief to his pocket. "I do beg your pardon, madam. Most rude of me."

"No one can help sneezing," Elizabeth assured him. She decided to give up asking him about the telephone. Violet would tell her if there was a message for her. As she turned toward the library, however, Martin said crossly, "If you are referring to those blasted contraptions in the kitchen and the study, I should like you to know there is something wrong with them."

Elizabeth paused. "There is? Oh, dear. Does Violet know that?"

"Dratted things keep making the most dreadful noise, jangling and clanging. I keep hearing them go off like fire engines. They must be broken. Nothing makes a noise like that unless it's broken."

Elizabeth sighed. "Martin, I've explained all that to you so many times. The telephone is supposed to make a noise. That's to let you know wherever you are in the house that someone wants to speak to you."

"In my day, madam, when someone wished to pay a call, they came to the house. They did not hide behind silly contraptions that make enough noise to wake the dead."

"Yes, well, things have changed, Martin, and we shall just have to get used to them."

"Change, change, that's all I hear nowadays." Martin began his agonizing shuffle toward the kitchen stairs. "What with people dashing around in motorized carriages, mechanical machines spitting bullets from the sky, Germans floating out of them with white umbrellas, and cowboys herding their cows all over the lawn and gardens, the whole world is rapidly going to pot, that's what I say."

Elizabeth felt sorry for him. In his confused state of mind, every minor irritation must seem like a catastrophe. Heaven knows what he'd do if they were invaded. Of course, if the Germans did invade Britain, people like Martin would be instantly eradicated. The Germans would have no use for anyone who could not pull his weight in their philistine vision of a new world.

She started as voices loudly erupted from the dining room. Recognizing Polly's shrill tones overlaying Violet's harsh commands, she hurried to intervene.

Polly stood at one end of the long, narrow room, feather duster in hand, while Violet paced up and down by the window. Both women were shouting at once, and Elizabeth had to raise her voice to be heard. Once a tense silence was restored, she looked at Violet. Two red spots burned in her housekeeper's cheeks, and her jaw jutted at a dangerous angle.

"I have never heard such insolence in all my life," she declared. "I don't know what the world is coming to, really I don't. When I was growing up, children were to be seen and not heard."

"When you were growing up, there were still bloody dinosaurs running around," Polly said rudely.

"That's enough, Polly!"

The sharp reprimand from Elizabeth got the girl's attention. She looked sulkily down at her foot and swished the duster over her shoe. "I'm doing the best I can. I don't have to work here, you know. I could get a job in the factory. They're crying out for workers down there."

"You're not old enough to work in the factory," Violet said, glaring at the hapless girl. "Nor intelligent enough, if you want my opinion."

"No one asked for your bloody opinion—" Polly began hotly, and once more Elizabeth intervened.

"Polly, go to the library and wait for me there."

For a moment it seemed as if she would refuse, then,

with a last baleful glare at Violet, she flounced from the room.

Elizabeth took the weight off her feet on the nearest chair. "What on earth was that all about?"

Violet shook her head and clicked her tongue. "That Polly, she'll be the death of me, that she will. Just because I told her she weren't to go nowhere near the Yanks when they got here. You'd have thought I'd told her to cut off her fingers, the way she carried on."

Elizabeth frowned. "Why can't she go near the Americans?"

"I should have thought that was obvious. We can't trust neither her nor them Yanks, that's why."

"I think we have to trust them. We can't take care of them without Polly's help. Unless you're prepared to pick up and clean up after them."

"What, me?" Violet tossed her head. "I have enough to do in the kitchen and whatnot, without running around after a bunch of bloody heathens."

Elizabeth's patience snapped. "Violet, I do wish you would stop referring to the Americans as if they were all brought up in caves. Those young men are risking their lives every day to help save our country from being taken over by the Germans. Every time a group of them take those airplanes up in the air, some of them don't come back. Most of them are barely old enough to drink. Imagine how you would feel if one of them were your son. The very least we can do is treat them with respect and consideration. We need the Americans. I don't think I have to remind you what would happen to us if England loses this war."

Violet puffed out her cheeks, looked as if she were about to argue, then let out her breath. "What is it, Lizzie? Are you all right? Did something happen?"

"Yes, I'm afraid something did happen." Elizabeth paused to take a deep breath. She felt ridiculously close to tears but wasn't quite sure why. "Beryl Pierce is dead. Her body washed up on the beach this morning."

"Oh, my dear Lord." Violet clutched her throat. "That poor child. And poor Winnie Pierce. She must be heartbroken. Does her husband know? How dreadful. I must get down there and see her."

"That would be nice, Violet. I'm sure she could use some company right now, and I have to go down to the police station this afternoon. I need to talk to George."

"My word, I bet he's all of a tizwoz. This is the biggest thing to happen to him since Walter Clapham got drunk and smashed all the windows in the town hall with a cricket bat. What do they think happened, then? Lost her way in the dark, I suppose. Not surprising, her riding that bicycle at night without a light. Never could understand how she could see where she was going. Course, a young girl like her hasn't got no right riding around late at night like that. If I were her mother—"

"Violet."

"Yes?"

"I do hope you'll keep your opinions to yourself when you see Winnie."

"Well, of course I will. I'll go down there this afternoon. Right after dinner. Polly can do the washing up for me. Speaking of which, I'd better get the dinner on. You haven't forgotten that Polly's waiting for you in the library, have you?"

"No, I haven't." Elizabeth got slowly to her feet. "Oh, by the way, Martin said the telephone rang while I was out."

"Oh, yes, it did. Forgot all about it, didn't I. It was that major from the American base. Said to tell you he'll be over first thing in the morning to talk about the arrangements for moving his men in to the Manor House."

Elizabeth felt a small quiver in the pit of her stomach. "Yes, all right, Violet. Thank you."

"Not at all, Lizzie. That's what I'm here for, isn't it." Violet gave her a sharp look, then headed out of the door, much to Elizabeth's relief.

She really had to stop these silly nerves whenever Major Monroe's name was mentioned, she told herself as she walked reluctantly down the hallway to deal with her rebellious maid. There would be enough to put up with once the men were billeted in the house without her having a fit every time she came in contact with their commanding officer.

Polly sat on the floor in front of the bookshelves, a book open on her lap. She closed it hurriedly when Elizabeth entered, then hoisted herself to her feet.

Elizabeth felt vaguely surprised. She didn't think there was anything on those shelves that would be remotely of interest to her maid. "I really don't want to hear you answering Violet back like that," she said as Polly replaced the book. "She is in charge of this house, and you must remember that."

"Yes, m'm." Polly looked suitably contrite.

"If you have any problems with her orders, you come to me, all right? Yelling and screaming at her like that only makes things more difficult."

"Yes, m'm."

"I know you'll have extra work when the Americans move in, but—"

"Oh, I don't mind that, honest I don't, Lady Elizabeth." Polly gazed up at her with earnest eyes. "I'll be happy to take care of them Yanks. It will be my duty, like, won't it. I'll be doing my bit for the war effort."

"Well, yes, I suppose so . . ."

"It were just that Violet said as how I wasn't to go near the Yanks, and that upset me. Like she didn't trust me or something."

"I'm sure she does trust you, Polly. She's just trying to protect you, that's all. Not that she has anything to protect you from," Elizabeth added hurriedly. "I'm quite sure the American officers are all perfect gentlemen."

"Yes, m'm. I expect they are." Polly's face seemed to glow with excitement. "It will be lovely having them here, Lady Elizabeth. They can get all sorts of things from the base. Cigarettes and whiskey and nylons and everything."

Elizabeth felt a twinge of anxiety. "Well, I really don't think we can expect anything like that. I sincerely hope you won't pester them, Polly."

"Oh, no, m'm. I wouldn't dream of it. Honest."

Elizabeth wished she could feel confident about that. "Well, run along, then, Polly. Violet probably needs your help in the kitchen."

"Yes, m'm. Thank you, m'm." Polly rushed to the door, then looked back over her shoulder. "And don't you worry about them Yanks, neither, Lady Elizabeth. I'll take really good care of them, you'll see." She disappeared, and Elizabeth could hear her humming all the way down the hallway. She wondered uneasily why that sounded so ominous.

After struggling through a plate of Violet's leftover stew, in which the lack of meat had been heavily supplemented with potatoes and bread, Elizabeth left the house and rode her motorcycle down to the town. She had rung George earlier to make sure he was there, though she wasn't sure how much he would tell her.

The rain had stopped, and several housewives had ventured out to do some shopping when she reached the High Street. A long queue of them waited outside Harold's, the greengrocer's, probably in the hopes of ensnaring one of the oranges that made all too rare an appearance these days. Every one of them waved at her as she sailed by.

Elizabeth parked her motorcycle next to the bicycles in the rack outside the police station, then pushed open the glass-fronted door. Sid Goffin's voice echoed from the back room. His anguished tones always sounded to Elizabeth as if he had a finger caught in a meat grinder.

George sat at the front desk and glanced up as she walked in. Without his police helmet, he looked like a benevolent monk. He was completely bald except for a thin strip of silvery hair that circled the back of his head. His round face bore few wrinkles, considering his advanced age, and with his bulging belly he reminded Elizabeth of a jolly Father Christmas, only without the whiskers.

There was nothing jolly about his expression, however, when he rose smartly to his feet and offered her a chair. He waited until she'd settled herself, then said carefully, "How can I help you, Lady Elizabeth?"

"It's about Beryl Pierce," she said, coming straight to the point. "I was wondering if there are any new developments. I'd like to know as many details as you can tell me."

She knew the instant she saw the change in his expression that there was more to Beryl's death than a simple accident. The trick, of course, was to get him to tell her what he knew. It would probably take all the diplomacy and tact she could muster. She could only hope she was up to the challenge.

CHAPTER
❀ 7 ❀

"I don't know as how I can tell you much at all, m'm,"
George said stiffly, "seeing as how it's police business,
that is. I really can't tell you anything until I've spoken
with the mother of the deceased and the next of kin have
been properly informed."

"I understand, George." Elizabeth peeled off her white
gloves. "You know how fast gossip circulates in the village. Everyone has their own ideas of what happened to
the poor child. I just thought it would be nice if I could
put their minds to rest." She looked the constable straight
in the eye. "We don't want to start a panic in the village,
do we."

"Panic, m'm? I'm not sure I rightly know what you
mean by that."

"There are some people who might think that Beryl
was pushed over that cliff. They might even start putting
the blame on the Americans."

73

"Well, m'm, human nature, isn't it. Seems to me, people will always find someone else to blame, and the Yanks are not exactly popular in the village. Ted Wilkins told me he has to throw a couple of them out of the Tudor Arms just about every night for causing an uproar with the British soldiers."

"And our soldiers are not in the least to blame, of course," Elizabeth said tartly.

George shrugged. "No doubt they do their share of aggravating. Boys will be boys, after all. Pardon me saying so, m'm, but I don't think there's much we can do about it. Them Yanks are going to get the blame for just about everything that happens around here, no matter who started it first."

Which was the very reason she should not jump to conclusions about the map found in Beryl's saddlebag, she reminded herself. "George," she said carefully, "I'm quite sure you realize how important it is for us all to remain on good terms with the Americans."

"As much as is possible, yes, m'm."

"Yes, well, that's why I need to know as much about Beryl's death as possible, so that I might contain the villagers if things get out of hand."

George looked alarmed. "Out of hand?"

"Well, there could be riots, fighting, that sort of thing. Very unpleasant. We need to avoid that at all costs."

"But, Lady Elizabeth, there's no one left to riot. Except for the army, and they've got military police to take care of that. The only people left in the village these days are mostly the old men, young children, and women."

"It's the women I am talking about, George. We have to realize that times have changed. Women drive tractors, build airplanes, and herd cows nowadays. They are quite capable of rioting. Surely you haven't forgotten the suffragettes? Are you sure you're prepared to confront fifty angry women armed with heavy iron frying pans advancing on the American base?"

George shuddered.

"She's right, George," Sid said from the doorway. "You should see my Ethel when she gets going. Like looking the bleeding devil in the face." He coughed. "Sorry, m'm. Didn't mean no disrespect."

"Not at all, Sid. I was just explaining to George that it's in all our best interests to share what information we have, so that we can work together to keep the people of Sitting Marsh calm and in control. I'm quite sure you two gentlemen have enough on your minds without having to spend your precious time pacifying a violent crowd of angry women."

"You're right about that, m'm," Sid said, nudging George in the shoulder. "We certainly don't want that, do we, George? I think we should share the information, really I do. After all, Lady Elizabeth is the lady of the manor. She should know what's going on in the village."

Elizabeth thought guiltily of all the clues lying in her bedroom. By rights she should pass them over to the constables. She was reluctant to do that just yet. She needed more time to ponder what they might mean, if anything, before giving them up to the incompetent manipulations of the local constabulary. Too much knowledge could be a very dangerous thing in the wrong hands.

"Well, I suppose we could give Lady Elizabeth some of the pertinent information without violating our procedures," George said, looking doubtfully at Sid, who nodded vehemently in response. "I could tell you, for instance, m'm, that Beryl wasn't exactly pushed over that cliff."

Elizabeth stared at him. Could all her instincts have

been wrong? Had the child committed suicide, after all? Somehow she found that hard to believe. "Wasn't pushed over? Are you saying she jumped?"

"Well, no, not exactly."

"Did she fall over, then?"

"She didn't jump, she didn't fall, and she wasn't pushed," Sid said gravely.

Elizabeth pursed her lips. This was going to be harder than she'd thought. "I see. So you're saying that Beryl didn't ride over the cliff on her bicycle, and that no one pushed her over."

"That's what I'm saying. Yes, m'm."

Elizabeth thought hard. "If she wasn't pushed, she didn't fall, and she didn't throw herself over the cliff, then what? Was she dropped out of an airplane or something?"

George hesitated. "In a manner of speaking, I suppose you could say that she was dropped, yes."

Obviously she would have to keep guessing until she got it right, Elizabeth thought on a rising tide of frustration. This was ridiculous. But necessary, if she was going to learn anything at all from these fools. "Was she conscious when she was . . . er . . . dropped?"

"No, m'm, she wasn't conscious." George shook his head. "And she didn't drown." He puffed out his chest. "There. I told you what didn't happen. That's not violating the procedure, is it?" He glanced at Sid for help.

"Not at all, George," Sid assured him.

It came to her all at once, snatching her breath away. "Beryl didn't drown. Of course. She was already dead, wasn't she?" Thoughts raced through her mind. "Oh, dear heaven. Poor Beryl was killed, then thrown over the cliff. And whoever did it tossed her bicycle over after her."

"Hit the nail right on the bloomin' head," Sid said solemnly.

"How was she killed? Stabbed? Clubbed with something?"

Again George gave a negative shake of his head.

Elizabeth searched her mind, trying to remember all the murder mystery books she'd read. "Shot? Strangled?"

George jerked his chin up and down.

"Beryl was strangled?" Elizabeth felt a distinct chill in spite of the stuffy warmth of the room. "Do you have any suspects?"

Again the negative shake of the head.

"Any clues at all that might help point to someone?"

Another shake.

Elizabeth sighed. "Does Winnie know yet?"

"No, m'm. I was going up there this evening, after I finish here."

Elizabeth's heart ached for the poor woman. "I wonder if you'd mind me taking the news to Winnie? It might help a little coming from me."

A look of immense relief crossed George's face. "I think that would be a very good idea, Lady Elizabeth. I'm much obliged."

"Not at all." Elizabeth rose to her feet, and George scrambled to get off his chair. "After all, the welfare of the villagers is my responsibility. I consider it my duty to do what I can to help in times of distress."

"Yes, m'm." George coughed. "Mind you, we don't have no idea how you came by this information, if you get my meaning?"

"Rest assured, George. Actually you didn't exactly tell me anything, now did you?"

"Once Mrs. Pierce is informed, of course, it won't remain a secret very long. But then it won't be us what's spreading the news around, and that's what's important."

"You know, of course," Elizabeth said, rising from her chair, "that once the North Horsham newspaper gets wind of this, someone will be down here demanding to know all the details."

George scrambled to his feet. "Well, m'm, he can demand all he likes, but he won't get them from us. Of course, there's nothing to stop him talking to the people in the village. Which is why I'd appreciate it, Lady Elizabeth, if you ask Mrs. Pierce to keep the details to herself for a while longer."

"I'll do that, George. Thank you."

Elizabeth strode down the steps, seething with frustration. All she'd been told was that Beryl had been strangled and her body thrown off the cliffs. There were no details. No clues, no suspects. Which made the whole charade just now somewhat pointless.

Once more she climbed aboard her motorcycle. But then again, the constabulary had their ways of doing things, and she had hers. She'd learned long ago that one had far more success if one respected other people's methods and worked with them instead of against them. Especially those people with any kind of authority.

Out of the blue a vision of Major Monroe's face popped into her mind. Good Lord, the man was becoming a positive obsession. With an impatient jerk of her wrist she revved up the engine of the motorcycle and roared down the High Street in the direction of Winnie's cottage.

According to Winnie, Violet had just left the cottage when Elizabeth arrived there. Winnie took one look at Elizabeth's face, then said quietly, "She was murdered, wasn't she?"

Elizabeth nodded unhappily. "I'm afraid it rather looks that way, yes. I'm so terribly sorry."

"How?"

"Winnie—"

"I want to know how she died." Apparently remembering whom she was addressing, Winnie muttered, "Begging your pardon, m'm."

"It's quite all right, Winnie. Understandable, under the circumstances. I understand Beryl was strangled and then thrown into the sea. Again, I'm so sorry."

Winnie shrugged. "No sense in dwelling on it, I suppose." She seemed to catch her breath. "Crying isn't going to bring her back, is it?"

"I suppose not. I do have one bit of good news." At Winnie's indication, Elizabeth made herself comfortable on the sofa. "George informed me that Stan is on his way home. Compassionate leave."

Winnie nodded, her lips pressed together. After a moment she said unsteadily, "I don't suppose they know who did it."

It was a statement more than a question, and Elizabeth sighed. "They have no suspects at the moment. I don't think George has ever handled a murder case before. I expect he'll call in an inspector."

"How long will that take?"

"I don't know. I imagine they are being kept very busy these days. So many policemen are joining up. That's the problem."

"I thought if they were police they didn't have to go," Winnie said, staring out of the window as if her mind was on something else entirely.

Which it probably was, Elizabeth thought, with a pang of sympathy. "They don't, but I suppose if they volunteer, the army is going to take them."

"Someone told me that all policemen have flat feet. That's how Evan never got in." She seemed to pull herself together. "I already told you that, didn't I."

"Winnie—"

"Lady Elizabeth, you've got to find out who did it. Please. By the time that inspector gets here, whoever did it could be miles away, and we'll never know the truth. I won't sleep nights until I know who killed my daughter and why."

Even if she hadn't already made up her mind to help, there was no way Elizabeth could deny this woman what she asked. "I'll do what I can," she said and prayed that it would be enough.

"I think it's this Robbie, whoever he is," Winnie said. She pulled a handkerchief from her apron pocket and blew her nose. "Find him and you'll find my daughter's murderer."

"Does . . . did Beryl have a girlfriend she was particularly close to?" It was still difficult for Elizabeth to realize that Beryl was dead. Heaven only knew how hard it was for Winnie.

"Amy Watkins. Those two have been friends since they were kids."

Elizabeth nodded. "Ah, of course. Amy. I've seen the two of them together many times."

Winnie looked hopeful. "You think she might know this Robbie?"

"We can certainly find out." Elizabeth rose to her feet. "I'll talk to her tomorrow. In the meantime, Winnie, try to get some rest. You look all in."

"I'm all right, m'm. But thank you."

"Can you manage on your own? Is there someone I can ask to stay with you?"

Winnie managed a weak smile. "No, thank you, m'm.

It's nice of you to offer, but I'd rather be alone right now."

"Very well, then." Elizabeth paused at the door. "If there's anything else I can do, please don't hesitate to call the manor."

"I will. Thank you, Lady Elizabeth. You will let me know just as soon as you hear anything?"

"The very minute," Elizabeth promised.

A feeling of intense weariness crept over her as she rode slowly back to the Manor House. It had been an exhausting day. She needed supper, then sleep, but first she wanted to go over the clues again. There had to be something there that would help her find Robbie, whoever he was. Then again, perhaps Amy could help her. She'd have to wait until tomorrow to talk to her.

Something else was happening tomorrow. Oh, yes. How could she have forgotten? Major Monroe was coming over to discuss the arrival of his officers. Everything happening at once.

She rather enjoyed Violet fussing over her when she returned. It was nice just to relax and let someone else take care of things for a change.

"I had a piece of Winnie's cake when I was there this afternoon," Violet announced when she brought in Elizabeth's evening glass of sherry. "It tasted good, considering it didn't have any eggs in it."

"I thought the same thing."

"I thought I'd give it a try. Winnie gave me the recipe."

"I think that's a marvelous idea. It's been so long since we had decent cake in the house." Elizabeth took a sip of the soothing liquid. She didn't know what she'd do without a glass of her favorite sherry now and again.

As if reading her mind, Violet said casually, "By the

way, there's only three bottles of sherry left in the cellar. I talked to Ted Wilkins at the Tudor Arms, but he said he didn't think they'd be getting any more for a while."

Elizabeth looked at her in dismay. "Three bottles? But that will be gone in no time. What are we going to do? There has to be somewhere we can get some."

Violet tipped her head to one side. "Well, now, Lizzie, it's none of my business, but it seems to me you could tap up that Major Monroe to get you some. Sort of payment for putting them all up. Don't you think?"

Elizabeth narrowed her eyes. "You're quite right, Violet. It is none of your business. I refuse to encourage anyone in this household to take advantage of the good nature of our guests."

"What if they want us to take advantage?"

"No sherry, Violet. No cigarettes, no chocolate, no nylons, no anything that comes out of that American base. Is that clear?"

Violet growled in her throat. "Seems to me that someone around here who's used to pulling strings and side-stepping the law might be a little more understanding about the matter."

"That's different."

"Oh, I see. It's not a matter of do what I do, but do what I say."

Elizabeth put down her glass. "Isn't it suppertime? I'm getting awfully hungry."

She winced as Violet swept from the room, letting the door slam behind her. She hated to argue with the one person she trusted above all others. Violet had been with the family since she was born.

Violet had been the one who'd stayed by her side day and night during that dreadful year when her parents had died and her marriage had fallen apart. It was Violet who had yelled at her when she refused to get out of bed and face another day. It was Violet who had given her back her self-esteem and her confidence, and it was Violet who had helped her gradually take over both her mother's and her father's duties and establish her rightful place in Sitting Marsh.

Violet, she knew, would get over her huff as swiftly as it had arisen. Her own stand was justified. Violet had spoken the truth when she'd accused her of sidestepping the proper channels at times. True, now and again she took advantage of her position to pull a few strings. But only when she'd exhausted the alternatives, and solely for the benefit of those unable to help themselves.

She just wasn't prepared to accept personal favors from the Americans, putting herself and her household in their debt. The Hartleighs had always taken care of their own, in good times and in bad. Just because there was a war on didn't mean she had to compromise her family's principles. Her father would never forgive her if she did. She would stand firm on her conviction. No matter what happened.

There were times when she missed her parents with an aching loneliness that nothing could appease. This quiet summer evening, with its deceptive air of calm and peace, was definitely one of those times.

CHAPTER

8

"Polly? Where is that girl?" Edna Barnett peeled the silver cap off the milk and rinsed it under the tap, then dropped the flattened disc into an Ovaltine jar that was already half full of tinfoil.

The young woman slouching at the kitchen table didn't bother to look up from the magazine in front of her. "She's upstairs, getting ready to go out."

"What again? She should be in bed, a girl her age, not gallivanting around town with all those bloody Yanks about."

"She's fifteen, Ma. She's a big girl."

"Not as big as she thinks she is, Marlene. I remember you at fifteen. That's what gave me all these blinking gray hairs." Edna carefully measured milk into a saucepan, then lit the gas underneath it.

" 'Ere!" Marlene lifted her head at that. "I never brought home no trouble."

"More by luck than judgment, I'd say. But then, you never had no Yanks hanging around you like a bunch of hungry wolves."

Marlene grinned. "What makes you think I don't now?"

Edna reached for a packet of rice. "You're eighteen. Old enough to know what you're doing, I hope."

"So's Polly, so stop worrying. Women grow up faster these days."

"Don't I know it." Edna measured rice into the bubbling milk. "Still, I don't want her hanging around them Yanks. Not a young girl like her. That's asking for trouble. Look what happened to that poor Beryl Pierce. Got herself blinking murdered, she did. That had to be a Yank."

"Who says so?" Marlene scowled at her mother. "Why does everyone blame the Yanks for everything what goes wrong around here?"

"Well, you tell me who else could have done it. All the English men have been called up. You know what Beryl was like, always throwing herself at the men. Though I shouldn't speak ill of the dead."

"Not all the men have been called up. Besides, what about the army camp in Beerstowe? Lots of them soldiers come to the village hall dance every month. Could have been any one of them. Could have been that Evan Potter she was going out with, for all we know."

"Evan?" Edna shook her head. "Don't make me laugh. He doesn't have the gumption for it. Couldn't even get in the army, could he. Nah, more likely to be one of them Yanks, that's what I say. And our Polly shouldn't be out late at night on her own. Her father would put a stop to it if he was here."

"Well, he ain't here, is he." Marlene folded up the

magazine and stood up. "He's in the bloody army. In any case, Polly's not going to be alone, is she. She's coming to the pictures with me."

Edna looked up in surprise. "With you? Why didn't you say so, then?"

Marlene grinned. "I like to see you get all worked up over nothing."

Footsteps clattered on the stairs, then Polly burst into the kitchen. "Come on, Marl, the picture will be starting before we get there if we don't hurry."

"I like that! You're the one what's been dithering about up there. I was ready ages ago."

"I had to draw the lines on me legs, didn't I. Are they straight?"

Marlene stared at the wavering seam lines painted down the back of her sister's legs. "Looks just like you're wearing real stockings."

"Wish I had real ones. Maybe I can get some off the Yanks when they move into the Manor House."

Marlene uttered a yelp. "The Yanks are moving into the Manor House? When?"

"Next week." Polly grinned. "And aren't I going to have a good time? Bet you wish you was me now, don't you. Surrounded by Yanks all day long. Pure blinking heaven."

"I can be around Yanks without having to work at the Manor House. All I have to do is go down the Tudor Arms on a Saturday night. Or the dance at the village hall. Or the High Street Odeon theater. I can have all the Yanks I want."

"Yeah? Well, none of that is like being in the same house with them."

"Well, I've been to the cricket pavilion with them, and that's as good as being in a house."

Edna threw her spoon down on the stove with a clatter loud enough to get both girls' attention. "Marlene Victoria Barnett! If I ever catch you talking about being in that cricket pavilion with a Yank again I'll lock you up every night for a month."

Marlene laughed. "You worry too much, Ma. They're just young boys. No different to English boys."

"Yeah," Polly agreed, "except they talk like Yanks and look gorgeous like Yanks and spend money like Yanks."

Both girls dissolved into giggles.

Yanks again. That's all she heard about nowadays. Edna sighed and gazed at her daughters. Polly took after her side of the family: skinny as a rat, pretty face, and jet-black hair. Marlene was more like her father, with her red hair and pale skin. She'd have a problem keeping her weight off when she got older, but right now she was well filled out. Just what the men went for these days.

The girls had grown up so fast. Didn't seem that long ago they were little, running around the kitchen getting under her feet. They'd been no trouble then. Now Polly was going to be working in a house full of trouble. Didn't bear thinking about.

"Bye, Ma!" Polly blew her mother a kiss.

"Won't be late," Marlene added, and the two of them disappeared into the hall.

Edna turned back to the stove and wished she'd had boys instead. But then she'd be worrying about them fighting the Germans. No one was safe these days. No one. Not even in a tiny village like Sitting Marsh.

Alone in her room, Elizabeth opened the wide windows that overlooked the back lawns. Thanks to double summertime, dusk settled late in the dying sunset, turning the birch trees into black silhouettes against the bloodred sky.

Beyond the tangled woods that bordered the Hartleigh land, the grassy slopes swept down to the cliffs, which rose steeply above wide, smooth stretches of golden sand. Three years ago summer visitors crowded the beaches, daydreaming in deck chairs or paddling in the gentle waves of the North Sea. Now the beaches lay empty year round. Ever since the fall of France and Belgium, in view of the serious threat of invasion from the Germans, the entire east coast had been heavily mined and the once-pristine cliffs disfigured with the ugly rolls of barbed wire.

On a night like this, however, with a fresh sea breeze filling her room with the salty fragrance of the ocean, Elizabeth could almost forget the unpleasant reminders of wartime. Closing her eyes, she listened to a distant blackbird warbling its late-evening song and imagined she was a child again, chasing Brandy across the lawns and into the woods.

That's what she needed, she decided, with a little rush of excitement. A dog. Two dogs. There hadn't been a dog in the Manor House since she'd left to marry and move to London. Dogs would give her the companionship she so sorely missed now that her parents were gone. She would see about it tomorrow. Or maybe the next day. She closed the windows with a snap and pulled down the black blinds. Major Monroe would be coming over tomorrow.

Banishing the little lift she felt at the thought, she plonked herself down on the bed and snapped on the bedside lamp. Clues. She needed to take another look at everything Winnie had given her before handing them over to George and Sid.

She opened the top drawer of her chest and drew out the box in which she'd carefully packed Beryl's belongings. Once more she spread them all out on the bed. The regimental pin gleamed in the soft light from her lamp, and she picked it up. The closest army camp was the Royal Artillery at Beerstowe. She'd seen the soldiers from there many times in the village. There could also be a Royal Engineers regiment stationed nearby. If so, she would have to find out where it was situated.

The map of America was badly creased and torn in one corner. It also, she discovered, had tiny holes around the edges. Apparently it had been pinned up on a wall. Not Beryl's, obviously, or Winnie would surely have seen it before. A wall at the American base? That seemed most likely. Someone must have given this map to Beryl. Robbie?

She picked up the letter. Two hearts had been drawn in the top right-hand corner, linked together, and underneath Robbie had scrawled, *"Be mine, and I'll be yours forever."*

Elizabeth laid the letter down and picked up the train ticket. Had Robbie also given Beryl a ticket to London? But that didn't make sense if he was stationed in Sitting Marsh. Unless he'd planned a romantic weekend. But then why a ticket for one way? And why would Beryl plan to go to London if she was thinking of joining the Land Army? The application stated quite clearly that she could expect to work on farms in the North Horsham area. Here in Norfolk. Not London.

Idly Elizabeth reached for the Land Army form and turned it over. A smudge of blue ink stained the blank sheet. It looked as if numbers had been scribbled there, but she could barely distinguish them. The form appeared to have been soaked by rain, washing out what might actually be a telephone number.

Excited at the prospect of another clue, Elizabeth held the sheet of paper under the lamp. The figures were so faint and smeared that she could only make out some of them. At least two of the numbers were illegible. Tomorrow, she decided, she would ring the various combinations and hope she connected with the right one.

Tomorrow, which now seemed full of possibilities.

With everything that was on her mind she really didn't expect to sleep well and was quite surprised when she woke up to find the morning sun streaming through the leaded windows. Anxious to begin her plan of action, she hurried through her usual routine. After much thought, she picked out a cream silk shirt to wear and her best linen skirt. Then she picked up the application form and stuffed it into her skirt pocket.

When she ran down to the kitchen, she found Violet sitting at the table, enjoying a cup of tea with the newspaper spread in front of her.

"What are you doing up with the lark?" she demanded when Elizabeth cheerily greeted her. "Got trouble sleeping?"

"I've got a busy day," Elizabeth reminded her. "I've been neglecting my duties. I still haven't paid the last week's bills, I have letters to write, and I should try to get down to the town hall this afternoon for the Ladies' Sewing Group meeting."

"Not to mention the meeting with the grievance committee."

Elizabeth stared at her in surprise. "What grievance committee?"

"I forgot to tell you." Violet folded the newspaper. "Ted Wilkins called early this morning. He wants to talk to you about a problem in the village. He's bringing Dier-dre Cumberland and Rosie Finnegan up here this after-noon."

Elizabeth pulled a face. "Oh, Lord. I can imagine what that will be about. It seems there's only one grievance on everyone's mind lately."

Violet got up from her chair. "Just wait until they find out the Yanks are moving in here."

Deciding to ignore her flash of irritation, Elizabeth sat down at the table. "Is there any tea in the pot?"

"Just made it. Read the paper while I get you a cup. Not that there's any good news. Looks like the Yanks are still fighting for their lives in them Pacific Islands."

Elizabeth scanned the headlines. It was hard to realize that the war was being fought on the other side of the world. It was all too easy to isolate oneself, concerned only with what happened on one's own doorstep. This madness wasn't confined to Europe anymore. The entire world was at risk, and that included a country as vast and as powerful as the United States of America. It was a sobering thought.

What was it Churchill had said after the Battle of Mid-way? The end of the beginning, and the beginning of the end. At times that end seemed very, very far away.

"I suppose you'll want me to prepare a meal for Major Monroe?" Violet placed a steaming cup of tea in front of Elizabeth. "We don't have much in the way of meat, but I could ask John Miller if he'd let me have one of his chickens. If you don't mind me indulging in a spot of black marketing, that is."

Noting the sarcasm in her housekeeper's voice, Eliz-abeth rattled the newspaper. "Not if you take him some of Daddy's best gin. Exchanges among friends are quite acceptable, I should think."

"Unless they're Americans, I take it."

Elizabeth sighed. She wasn't quite sure why she made such a sharp distinction between the locals and the Americans. Maybe it was the way the young girls threw themselves at the airmen, forsaking their boyfriends who were overseas, fighting for their lives in the trenches.

Maybe it was the resentment in the village from some of the older women, and especially from the men who were left, who considered the Americans a threat to every woman in Sitting Marsh.

Overpaid, oversexed, and over here. It was the battle cry all over the village, and probably in every other village, town, and city paying host to the American military. It wasn't fair, of course, but understandable. The British girls were being swept off their feet by the glamorous Yanks, and there didn't seem much anyone could do about it.

Yet these same men—boys, most of them—were putting their lives on the line every day for the very people who condemned them. Every day the planes flew out from the base, and every day less and less of them came back. For that reason alone, she would do anything she could to see that the American officers were as comfortable as she could make them. But she would not accept favors from them.

The Hartleigh pride was at stake, she assured herself. It had absolutely nothing to do with her sworn vow never to lose her head over a man again. All right, so there was something about the Americans that she found intriguing. Or at least one in particular. Nevertheless, she was not about to join the hordes of adoring women who apparently were desperate to keep company with any man wearing the irresistible uniform of the United States Army Air Force.

"What in heaven's name are you cooking up in that mind of yours?" Violet demanded, startling Elizabeth out of her thoughts. "You've got a furrow deep enough in your forehead to grow potatoes."

"I was just thinking about our preparations to house the Americans." She avoided Violet's sharp eyes. "All those portraits in the great hall will have to be dusted, the chimneys in the east wing will have to be swept. . . . There's so much to be done."

"I suppose we should do something about the plumbing over there, too." Violet opened a cupboard and took down a tin of porridge. "The way that water rattles in those pipes you'd think it was Old Marlowe coming after Scrooge with his Christmas ghosts."

"It's not the water that rattles, it's the air in the pipes."

"Whatever it is, if we don't get it seen to, them Yanks will think this house is haunted."

Elizabeth watched her measure the oatmeal into a pan. "Those men risk their lives to fly their planes into enemy fire every single day," she observed quietly. "I really don't think a few rattles in the pipes are going to disturb them. Besides, we can't afford it."

"We can't afford no chimney sweeps, neither. That's if we could find one, and I doubt that. Anyone young enough and healthy enough to climb over these roofs has been called up by now."

"Then we shall have to clean them ourselves."

Violet spun around to face her. "Have you forgotten what happened when you decided we should mend the drainpipe ourselves? Maybe that bump you got on your head wiped it out of your mind."

"I fell off the ladder because the ground was soft from the rain."

"Exactly. And what happened when you insisted on

painting the ceiling in the library yourself?"

"I never did like that chandelier much." Elizabeth smiled. "Come now, Violet, admit it. You enjoy the challenge just as much as I do."

"I like living in one piece, too. Hanging from a chandelier with one hand is not my idea of fun."

"I forgot the library ladder has wheels on it."

"You'll break your neck one of these days, Lizzie. You mark my words. The master would turn in his grave if he knew half of what you're up to around here."

"You fuss over nothing, Violet. Besides, it isn't cold enough to worry about lighting fires yet. We still have time to decide what to do about the chimneys." Elizabeth wrinkled her nose. "Can I smell burning?"

Violet gave a yelp and made a grab for the pot. "Look at that now. Caught it on the bottom."

"That's all right. I like it burned."

"Just as well, because that's the way you've got it this morning."

Elizabeth laughed. "I don't think either Daddy or Mother would worry, knowing you are here to take care of me."

"You need someone to take care of you, and that's a fact," Violet muttered, but Elizabeth could tell she was pleased with the comment.

Actually, if her mother were here, she'd probably be horrified at the familiarity that had developed between her daughter and the housekeeper. *One does not waste time in idle chatter with the servants. Too much familiarity breeds contempt.* She could just hear her mother's voice expressing her disapproval. They did things differently in the old days, she would say. But this wasn't the old days. The war had changed everything.

Even the king and queen had visited the bombed-out

ruins of East London and talked to the people on the streets. Unheard of before the war. Nowadays people lived for each day, grateful to survive. They were all in this together. There was something rather comforting about that.

As soon as she'd finished her breakfast, Elizabeth hurried to the study and closed the door. She was anxious now to try the telephone numbers she'd found on the application form.

Seated at her rolltop desk, she traced as best she could the smudged numbers on the back. The two she had to guess she left blank. Starting with a one, she substituted the blanks and dialed a number. The high-pitched rapid buzzing told her it was unobtainable. The next number she dialed gave her the same result. On the third try, a woman answered the telephone.

"I'd like to speak with Beryl Pierce, please," Elizabeth said quickly. It was the first thing that came to mind. She should have given this more thought.

"There's no one of that name here," the woman said, sounding apologetic. "Is she a novice?"

Elizabeth blinked. "I beg your pardon?"

"Perhaps you have the wrong number," the woman suggested. "This is the convent in East Common."

"I think I do have the wrong number," Elizabeth said faintly. "I do beg your pardon." She replaced the receiver and frowned at the smudges. Now that she really looked at the numbers, one of the blanks looked a bit like a five. She tried dialing again. Unobtainable. Thank heavens the North Horsham exchange had switched to automatic dialing a couple of years ago. She would have driven an operator crazy. Twice more she dialed, and then the call went through.

The woman on the end of the line answered with a

voice of efficiency. "Ministry of War, Land Army Recruitment Center. Can I help you?"

It wasn't often Elizabeth felt foolish. Right now she felt like the biggest nitwit of the century. The telephone number on the back of the Land Army application was for the recruitment office. Of course. Any idiot could have realized that.

She dropped the receiver in its cradle without answering the voice. There was no point in asking about Beryl, since she hadn't filled out the application. Idly she turned the form over, already trying to decide when she should talk to Beryl's friend, Amy.

There was the name of the recruitment center in bold black letters, with the telephone number printed underneath. So why was it scribbled on the back? She turned the sheet of paper over and examined the smudged number on the back of the form again. The numbers were different. Which meant that whoever answered the telephone just now wasn't in the general office of the recruitment center. She had to be in a private office.

With rising hope, Elizabeth dialed the number again. The same woman answered, sounding a trifle impatient. Deciding to take no chances, Elizabeth said cautiously, "I was given this number by an associate. To whom am I speaking?"

"This is Carol Simmons, recruitment officer. Can I help you?"

"Er . . . yes, this is a friend of Beryl Pierce. She gave me your number to call."

After a slight pause, the voice asked cautiously, "Were you interested in joining the Land Army?"

"No . . . er . . . that is—"

"You have to come to the recruitment center and fill out an application. We're in the High Street, on the corner of Williams. Hours are ten till four." The line clicked and went dead.

Elizabeth replaced the receiver. Obviously Carol Simmons didn't deal with applicants by telephone. So how did Beryl get her number? Either she knew her personally or she went to the office to talk to her about joining up. The chances were this woman knew nothing more than the bare facts about her. Then again, Beryl could have recounted her entire life history during the conversation. If she had, there might be something there that could help point a finger in the right direction.

There was only one way to find out. It was all too easy to cut someone off when you didn't want to answer questions on the telephone. It was much more difficult to avoid those questions when sitting face-to-face with someone.

Tomorrow she would go to the recruitment center, Elizabeth decided, and somehow she would bring Beryl into the conversation. Her efforts might be a waste of time and not lead anywhere, of course, but if Carol Simmons knew Beryl personally, she might also know the mysterious Robbie. Elizabeth was very anxious indeed to talk to that young man. She had the feeling that Robbie, whoever he was, might well be able to shed some light on the untimely death of a young girl.

CHAPTER
✿ 9 ✿

Elizabeth spent the next two hours catching up on her bookkeeping and correspondence. She was on her way back to her room when she encountered Martin in the hallway. "I have a message for you, madam," he said, drawing his frail body up as straight as his stooped shoulders would allow.

"Yes, Martin?"

He stared at her over the rims of his glasses. "Madam?"

"You have a message for me?"

After another long pause, he scratched his head. "Darned if I know."

"Think, Martin," Elizabeth said gently. "Was it something Violet wanted me to know?"

"Violet? Well, now that you come to mention it, madam, I think it was. Yes. Violet. That was it."

"And what did she want you to tell me?"

Again the blank expression.

"Perhaps I should ask her myself."

"I think that might be a very good idea." Martin nodded his head up and down. "I'll tell the gentleman that you have been detained."

Elizabeth's heart skipped a beat. "Which gentleman?"

"The one in the drawing room. I told him to wait in there because you were in the study and I didn't think you should be disturbed."

"Major Monroe? He's here?"

Martin looked confused. "Didn't I announce him?"

"Of course, Martin." Elizabeth patted his arm. "I just forgot. I'll go right away."

"What about Violet, madam? Shall I tell her you'll be along later?"

"Please do. And ask her to send Polly up with some tea and biscuits, please."

"Yes, madam."

Martin shuffled away, and Elizabeth took a deep breath. First she had to still the rapid beating of her heart, then she had to remind herself that men in general were not to be trusted or believed.

Thus armed and protected, she pushed open the door of the drawing room. The man seated in the armchair rose to his feet as she entered. His cap lay on the table next to him, next to what appeared to be a bottle wrapped in brown paper.

"Major Monroe," she said hurriedly, "I apologize for keeping you waiting. My butler has only just informed me of your presence."

"That's just fine, ma'am." He swept a hand at the room. "I've been looking at some of your antiques. You have some interesting stuff here."

"Er . . . yes, thank you. Most of them have been in my family for generations."

"I particularly like that sword hanging up there."

Following his gaze to the saber hanging on the wall above the fireplace, Elizabeth smiled. "My grandfather carried that during the Boer War."

"No kidding." Earl Monroe gazed at it a moment longer, then reached for the package. "With my compliments, ma'am."

Flustered, Elizabeth shook her head. "Oh, I couldn't. I mean, that isn't necessary. Really."

"It's just a bottle of sherry, ma'am. Little enough for letting a mess of strangers into your home."

"Oh, it's really not that much trouble. One has to do what one can for the war effort."

"I'd like you to have it."

He held the bottle out to her, and good manners made it impossible for her to refuse. Feeling like a traitor to her own convictions, she took the package and opened it. "Cream sherry. How terribly decent of you. Thank you so much, Major."

"Earl. And you're welcome, ma'am."

"Right." She put the bottle down before he saw the slight tremble of her hand. "Well, I suppose we should discuss the arrangements for your men. How many will there be, exactly?"

"Nine, all told. I hope that won't be too much for you?"

"Nine? No, I don't think so. Though they might have a tight squeeze in the beds."

Earl Monroe smiled. "I reckon we can take care of that, Lady Elizabeth. We'll be bringing in cots for the men. And lockers."

"Oh, right." She felt out of breath, as if she'd been

running up Mistletoe Hill. What a ridiculous thought. She couldn't run up it even when she was a child. "Now, about meals?"

"We'll be eating mostly on the base with the rest of the men. We'll be out on missions a good part of the time, anyway. Weather permitting, of course."

"Oh." She stared at him, unsettled by his words. "I hadn't realized that army majors go on bombing missions."

"Army Air Force, ma'am. We're all qualified to fly. And these days we need every man we can get."

"Yes, I suppose so. I just hadn't thought . . ." Her stomach churned, and she made an effort to smile. "Well, then, if you have any more questions?"

"If it wouldn't be too much trouble, ma'am, I'd like to see the quarters again."

"Quarters? Oh, you mean the east wing. Of course." She turned to leave, then paused abruptly when the major stepped smartly in front of her and opened the door. "Thank you." At least the man had manners, she thought as she sailed past him. It seemed, as she'd always maintained, that not all Americans were heathens after all.

Walking down the great hall with Major Monroe following a few steps behind turned out to be an unsettling experience.

She was quite relieved when he paused in front of a portrait, asking, "Is this one of your ancestors?"

"They all are. The gentleman you are looking at was my great-great-grandfather. He was seventeen when he fought at Balaklava during the Crimean War."

"Well, isn't that something." Earl Monroe studied the oil painting. "The Charge of the Light Brigade. Alfred, Lord Tennyson."

"That's right!"

She'd been unable to hide her astonishment, and he shrugged. "Majored in English in college."

Now she was really impressed. "Really? Where did you go to college?"

"University of Wyoming, ma'am."

Elizabeth considered that. "Isn't there some kind of park in Wyoming?"

It was his turn to look surprised. "Yellowstone. Yes, ma'am. First place to be designated as a national park."

"And mountains. The Rockies?"

He grinned, suddenly looking years younger. "Reckon you paid attention in class."

"I was always interested in geography." She moved on, feeling inordinately pleased. A thought occurred to her, and she paused, deciding she might as well take advantage of the opportunity. "Speaking of geography, I have a map that I believe might have come from your base. If you wouldn't mind waiting here for a moment, I'll fetch it."

"Take your time." He gazed up at the row of portraits. "I'd like to take a closer look at some of these paintings."

She hurried off, leaving him to bask in the presence of her heritage. It took her just a few minutes to retrieve the map from her room and return with it. She found him contemplating a portrait of her great-aunt Rebecca, a stern-faced woman laced painfully into a restrictive gown of the Victorian era.

"Tough-looking dame," he commented when she reached his side.

"She was. She brought up nine children single-handedly. She was fifty-two when she died in prison."

"Prison?"

She almost laughed at his shocked expression. "She was a suffragette. She was arrested and put in prison, went on a hunger strike, and starved to death. I was only about three years old at the time, but I vaguely remember all the fuss when she died."

His intense gaze on her face made her squirm. "Interesting family you have there."

"You don't know the half of it. One of these days when you have more time I'll tell you all about my great-great-uncle Matthew. His adventures at sea would make a wonderful novel."

The crinkles at the corners of Major Monroe's incredible eyes deepened. "I'd like that. You've got a date."

Flustered, she didn't know how to answer him. To cover her confusion she began walking rapidly toward the master suite. "You should be able to fit some cots in here." She threw open the door. "There's the bed, of course. I don't know what you want to do about that."

She stood to one side so he could look in at the heavy four-poster bed that had been in her family for more than a century.

"I reckon I'll be able to make good use of that."

Quickly she banished the image of the major lying full length on the bed from her mind. "Good. Then we have three more bedrooms, but they each have one bed in them. Unless your men don't mind sleeping together, I suppose you'll have to supply the other beds."

"We'll take the beds down and bring in our own cots." He glanced down the hallway. "You have one bathroom, right?"

"Yes, I'm afraid so. Is that going to present a problem?"

"No, ma'am. Not at all. The men will appreciate having a real bathroom again."

"Well, I should warn you," she said as she closed the bedroom door and headed down the hall, "the pipes make a bit of a noise. I haven't been able to find a plumber since Brian Finch went into the navy. He used to do all our work in the manor." She didn't add that she couldn't have afforded Brian's services even if he'd been there, thanks to Harry Compton and his despicable gambling habit.

"Please quit worrying so much about us, Lady Elizabeth. The men are used to far worse, I promise you."

"I want things to be comfortable for you."

He smiled, destroying her composure once more. "Just being allowed to stay in a house like this is a privilege. Believe me, we'll be more than comfortable."

She let out her breath. "All right, then. So, when will you be moving in?"

"Next week. Monday, if that's okay with you?"

Elizabeth did some frantic calculations in her head. "I think we can be ready by then."

"Lady Elizabeth, I'm begging you, don't make a big deal out of this, okay? I feel guilty enough as it is, having to dump my men on you like this. I'll do my level best to see they don't take advantage of your great hospitality."

"It's no trouble at all," Elizabeth assured him, thinking about the fireplaces to be swept. Thank heavens it was still warm, though with only a month until September, the winds from the North Sea would turn the nights chilly soon enough.

She dug a hand into her pocket and contacted the smooth folds of paper. She'd forgotten about the map. "Oh, here's the map I was telling you about." She drew it from her pocket and handed it to him. "I am right, aren't I? It did come from your base?"

Major Monroe examined it, turning it over in his hands. "Sure looks like it. Where did you get it?"

"Well, that's something I rather wanted to talk to you about." She started walking with him back down the great hall, conscious of their footsteps echoing from the vast ceiling above them. "I'm afraid we've had a tragic turn of events in the past couple of days. A young girl was found strangled on the beach."

"Yes, ma'am. I heard about it. Lousy business. I hope it wasn't a friend of yours?"

"The daughter of a friend," Elizabeth said quietly.

"Aw, gee, I'm sorry."

"Thank you. Anyway, this map was found in the saddlebag of her bicycle, and I was just wondering . . ." She let her voice trail off as she saw his expression change.

"If one of my men did it," he finished for her, his voice turning distressingly harsh. "Just because she had a map from the base? She could have gotten this map anywhere and from anyone."

Aware that she was treading on sensitive ground, Elizabeth hastened to reassure him. "Yes, of course, Major. I'm not accusing anyone. As far as I know, there are no suspects in the case. I was merely trying to establish if Beryl was acquainted with someone from the base, and if so, perhaps the man could in some way help us find out what happened the day she was killed."

They reached the end of the great hall, and the major paused at the head of the stairs. "Correct me if I'm wrong, ma'am, but it seems to me that this is a job for the police."

It was a mild rebuke, but a rebuke nevertheless. Dismayed by the sudden tension that she sensed between them, Elizabeth did her best to make amends. "Major Monroe, I do hope you don't think I was singling out one of your men. A young girl has died at the hands of a killer, and so far no one seems to have any clues as to the identity of the murderer. Her mother has begged me to find out what I can, and as lady of the manor, it is my duty to help my people. I'm simply trying to do my duty."

She'd expected that he, of all people, would understand her obligation, but apparently her plea fell on deaf ears.

"Then I wish you luck with it," he said dryly. "Now I really should be getting back to the base."

She followed him down the stairs, berating herself for the way she'd handled things. If they were all to survive the invasion of the Americans in the Manor House, it was imperative that she remain on good terms with their leader. Communication was going to mean everything in the weeks or months ahead.

She waited for him to retrieve his cap from the drawing room, then accompanied him to the front door. "Thank you for calling in, Major. We shall expect you next Monday, then?"

He pulled on his cap, then gave her a casual salute. "Next Monday, Lady Elizabeth. Bright and early."

"Bright and early," she muttered under her breath as she closed the door. They'd probably arrive at the crack of dawn. It wasn't until she was halfway across the entrance hall before she realized that Polly never did bring the tea and biscuits.

Still smarting from the awkward encounter with the major, she took the map back to her room. Before putting it back in the box with the other things, on impulse she opened it and spread it out on the bed.

After a moment or two she found Wyoming on the western half of the map. Such a big country, she thought, idly tracing her finger across to New York, which was the first place most British people thought of at the mention of America. Either that or Hollywood.

Something caught her eye, and she moved her finger back. A small red circle had been drawn near the east coast on the map. She took a closer look. The circle enclosed a town called Camden, in the state of New Jersey.

Elizabeth stared at the circle. If Robbie was an American, could this be his hometown? If so, it could be a way of finding him. She couldn't just go wandering onto the base, however, asking questions about a man named Robbie from Camden, New Jersey. She would need help. Major Monroe's help. The question was, in view of the recent disagreement, if one could call it that, whether or not the major would consent to help her at all.

She felt sad, as if she'd lost something special. Which was ridiculous, of course. One couldn't lose what one had never had. Nevertheless, she couldn't shake the vague feeling of depression, and that worried her more than anything.

She decided to cure her misplaced melancholy by paying Amy Watkins a visit. Amy was Beryl's best friend. If Major Monroe wouldn't help find Robbie, then maybe Amy could tell her where to find him. It was worth a try, at least, and it would give her something else to think about, other than a tall, vital American with entirely too much charisma for her peace of mind.

CHAPTER
❧ 10 ❧

Early that afternoon, as Elizabeth sat in her study attempting to organize her filing cabinet, she heard the clanging of the doorbell echo through the hallway. She waited, poised to rise, should Martin not reach the front door in a reasonable amount of time.

A few moments later a noisy commotion erupted, and upon investigating, she found Martin braced on the front doorstep insisting the visitors hand over their calling cards.

Ted Wilkins, who suffered from asthma, no doubt due to residing in the thick fog of cigarette smoke that incessantly filled his pub, wheezed so alarmingly Elizabeth considered ringing Dr. Sheridan, while Deirdre Cumberland argued in a shrill tone most unbecoming for a vicar's wife. The third member of the little group seemed more interested in the stray wisps of her hair tugged free by the brisk wind. Rosie Finnegan worked at the clothing shop in the High Street and was constantly absorbed by her appearance.

After reassuring Martin and sending him on his way, Elizabeth showed her guests into the library and prepared herself for the worst.

Ted Wilkins, having regained his breath now that he'd calmed down, opened with the first shot. "We've been holding some meetings in the town hall, Lady Elizabeth, and we three have been elected to represent the rest of the villagers. They want you to do something about those Yanks. They're causing nothing but trouble in Sitting Marsh."

"They really are becoming a nuisance." Deirdre glanced around the room as if she were inspecting the furniture for dust. "You can't go anywhere now without seeing them lounging around on the street corners, molesting any young girl who happens to walk by."

"Bloody lecherous they are, m'm," Rosie agreed. "Think they're all blinking Casanova."

Elizabeth rather suspected that this was the usual case of sour grapes. Ted had always fancied himself as a ladies' man, in spite of being vastly overweight. Until the Americans moved onto their base, he'd had little competition from the few men left in town. Dierdre, although well past the age of fifty, still dressed in girlish frocks and hats as if trying to recapture her lost youth, while Rosie, a divorcée whose lack of morals had always been a source of gossip, was most likely competing with girls half her age for attention.

"I really don't see what I can do about it," Elizabeth said, trying to sound reasonable. "The Americans are here to stay until this war is over, and we must all remember they are here to help us, and they deserve our compassion and respect."

"It's a little hard to respect a bunch of hooligans when they are whistling and shouting obscene remarks to every woman who passes," Deirdre said stiffly.

"They are young boys, most of them. No different from our own boys at that age."

"They're in a foreign country," Ted said, beginning to wheeze again. "They should respect our women."

"Perhaps they would," Elizabeth said quietly, "if those women didn't deliberately lead them on. I've seen the girls in the village, and frankly, the way some of them dress and behave, I'm surprised these young men have as much restraint as they've shown so far."

"I hope you're not looking at me when you say that, m'm," Rosie said indignantly.

Trying not to think about wearing the shoe that fits, Elizabeth said firmly, "I'm not inferring anything at all, Rosie. I'm trying to be fair, that's all. I do believe that instead of finding fault and making accusations, we would all benefit if we welcomed these young men and made allowances for their high spirits. After all, considering the dreadful risks they are taking in order to help us, I should think the least we can do is try to get along with them. Most of them are lonely, scared, and incredibly brave. They deserve our compassion and our friendship."

"Well, what about this murder, then?" Ted demanded. "Does the murderer of a young girl deserve our compassion and friendship?"

Elizabeth straightened in her chair. "There is no evidence at all that points to an American being responsible for this terrible crime. Until we know more about the matter, I think it would be very unwise to assume anything about anyone."

"Well, I wouldn't trust those Yanks farther than I could throw them," Rosie said, tossing her bleached curls.

"But that's exactly what we have to do if we're going to live in harmony with them. To that end, in fact, I've agreed to house several of the American officers here at the Manor House."

Three pairs of shocked eyes stared at her.

"Oh, dear," Deirdre muttered, "that will put the cat among the pigeons for certain."

"With all due respect," Ted mumbled, "I hope you know what you're doing, m'm."

Rosie simply sat there, apparently stunned by the news and probably green with envy, Elizabeth thought smugly.

"I'm quite confident everything will run smoothly," she assured Ted. "Well, now, is there anything else I can help you with?"

For the next twenty minutes or so she listened to the various minor complaints and concerns of the three delegates and promised to do what she could, even though she knew the main purpose of their visit had not been resolved. As long as the Americans remained in the vicinity of Sitting Marsh, it seemed likely there would be some dissent among the villagers. All she could hope was that things wouldn't get out of hand to the point where drastic measures would have to be taken. And pray that Beryl's murderer was not stationed on the American base.

Later that afternoon Elizabeth rode her motorcycle out along the coast road to where a small group of thatched cottages ringed the harbor. Mickey Watkins would still be out on the ocean, and Elizabeth wanted to talk to his daughter before the sour-tempered fisherman returned.

When she arrived, Jessie Watkins was hanging sheets

on the line to dry. The fisherman's wife nervously greeted her visitor and invited her into the cramped sitting room.

"Amy isn't home yet, m'm," she said in response to Elizabeth's query. "She shouldn't be too long, though. I have some fresh currant buns if you'd like one or two while we're waiting?"

She left Elizabeth alone to contemplate the flowered wallpaper while she made a pot of tea and toasted buns under the gas grill. Reminded of the incongruous pattern covering the wall in what would be Major Monroe's bedroom, Elizabeth wished heartily that her mother's taste had been less flamboyant.

When the fisherman's wife returned, she was carrying a tray bearing a pot of tea and a half dozen currant buns, which no doubt had taken up her entire ration of sugar and butter for the week. Having assured herself her visitor had everything she needed, she sat herself down on a faded velvet armchair and picked up a length of knitting from a footstool sitting next to her.

"I expect you've come about Beryl," she said, just when Elizabeth was about to broach the subject herself. "Terrible, that was. Such a young girl and all. Amy was with her just last week."

"It must have been an awful shock for Amy." Elizabeth put her empty plate down beside her cup and saucer. "They've been friends for so long."

"Most of their lives. Things will never be the same again for our Amy, that's for sure. What with her brothers in the navy now, and her best friend gone, she's feeling really alone. I worry about her. I don't want her turning to the Yanks for company. God knows what that will lead to. You hear such stories nowadays. Sitting

Marsh isn't the place it used to be, not with foreigners coming in and running around murdering people."

Elizabeth did her best to hide her resentment. It seemed that all she did lately was defend the Americans against unfair accusations. "We can't really blame anyone until we know for sure who did this ghastly thing."

"Well, who else would it be, m'm?" Jessie's needles clicked furiously. "We never had any trouble before those Yanks came into town. Nice and peaceful it was before they got here."

Time to change the subject, Elizabeth decided. "How are your boys? Have you heard from them?"

"Don't hear much from them. Not allowed to say much, are they. What they do say they tell me not to repeat. Loose lips sink ships. That's what they're always telling me."

"Very true." Through the open window Elizabeth heard the creak of Jessie's garden gate.

Jessie must have heard it, too. The clacking of her needles stopped. She folded her knitting and tucked it into the cloth bag. "That'll be our Amy now, m'm," she said, and got to her feet with an air of relief. "I'll tell her you're here."

Elizabeth waited while the soft murmur of voices wafted in from the hallway. Finally a tall, thin girl with short, stringy brown hair appeared in the doorway.

"Good afternoon, Lady Elizabeth." Amy kept her eyes down and ground the toe of her shoe into the carpet. "Mum said you wanted to speak to me."

"Come and sit down, Amy." Elizabeth patted the seat next to her on the sofa, but Amy threw herself down on the armchair her mother had just vacated.

"I don't know nothing about what happened to Beryl," she burst out.

Elizabeth could tell she was on the verge of tears. "You must miss her very much," she said gently.

Amy nodded, her thin lips pinched so hard they almost disappeared.

"I'm sorry, Amy. I know this is upsetting for you, but we have to find out who did this awful thing to her. Beryl would want that, don't you think?"

Amy nodded again.

"I know you don't want to talk to P.C. Dalrymple about this, but if I don't find out what happened to Beryl, sooner or later he'll be coming around asking questions."

This time Amy's eyes widened in dismay.

"Perhaps you can tell me something that will help me, so that he won't have to question everybody."

Finally the girl spoke, her voice trembling so violently Elizabeth felt quite concerned for her. "I'll try, Lady Elizabeth, but I don't know nothing. Honest."

The words were soft and indistinct, but it was at least an answer. "Amy, have you ever heard Beryl speak about someone named Robbie?"

A violent shake of the head accompanied Amy's answer. "No, m'm. I never heard of no one by that name."

"Did she ever mention going out with an American?"

"A Yank?" Amy looked shocked. "No, m'm, that I do know. Beryl would never dare go out with a Yank."

Surprised, Elizabeth stared at her. She didn't want to be uncharitable to the poor deceased girl, but surely Amy knew that Beryl would have welcomed with open arms an advance from any man. Literally. "Why wouldn't she be interested in the Americans?" she asked cautiously.

Amy uttered a shaky laugh. "Beryl was really interested in them. She would have loved to go out with one.

But she was afraid of her dad. Her mum told her that if she went anywhere near that base she'd tell Beryl's father, and he'd give it to her when he got home."

Elizabeth didn't think that would be enough to stop Beryl doing what she wanted.

She was about to say so when Amy added, "Besides, m'm, Beryl would never two-time Evan. He'd beat up anyone who looked at her."

Shocked, Elizabeth stared at her. "Evan? Did Beryl tell you that?"

Amy nodded. "Yes, m'm. He was so rough on Steve, Beryl said, Steve's face looked like a piece of raw meat when he'd finished with him. Evan told Beryl he'd do the same to anyone who came near her. That's how I know Beryl would never go out with a Yank. It would have caused too much trouble for everyone."

Elizabeth barely heard the last part of Amy's declaration. She was too busy concentrating on something else she'd said. "Steve? Is he a friend of Beryl's?"

Amy looked frightened. "I don't know his last name, honest. I never met him. He's a soldier. Stationed in London."

The owner of the regimental badge, perhaps? Elizabeth felt a stirring of excitement. "And Beryl was going out with Steve?"

"Well, I don't know as if you could call it going out, m'm. Beryl met him in North Horsham, around Easter time. He'd come down to visit a mate of his who was stationed out at Beerstowe. Anyway, Beryl started writing to him, then about two months ago, middle of June it were, Steve came down here again to see Beryl. Well, Evan found out about it, didn't he. Went looking for him and beat him up. When Beryl saw him, just before he went back to London, she said she hardly recognized him, his face were that bad."

"I see." So that was why Evan had that peculiar look on his face when she'd mentioned the regimental badge. Especially since she'd called the soldier Robbie instead of Steve. Elizabeth found it impossible to believe that quiet, soft-voiced Evan could have give anyone a vicious beating. "Do you know where Steve was stationed?"

"No, m'm. Beryl never told me anything like that."

"Did Beryl see Steve again after Evan fought with him?"

Amy shrugged. "Not that I know of, but then, Beryl never told me everything. She was sort of secretive about what she did. I think she was afraid I'd tell her mum."

"I see. Well, thank you, Amy." Elizabeth rose to her feet. "I'm sorry if talking about Beryl has upset you, but if I'm to find out what happened to her, these questions are necessary."

"Will P.C. Dalrymple be coming here, then?" Amy asked, her voice quivering again.

"I suppose it all depends on how much I can find out first." Elizabeth drew on her gloves. "Don't worry, Amy. If the constable asks you any questions, just tell him what you told me."

"Yes, m'm. Thank you, Lady Elizabeth."

Elizabeth left the cottage feeling a little guilty. She wondered if what she was doing could be construed as interfering with a police investigation. Though all she was really doing was asking questions. *And withholding evidence in the form of clues,* her conscience reminded her.

Well, everything would be all right when she found out who strangled Beryl and threw the poor girl over the cliffs. George would no doubt thank her for saving him all that time and effort. Clinging to that faint reassurance, she set off back to the manor.

On the way up the winding lane, it occurred to her that the soldier named Steve could have been the reason Beryl bought the train ticket. Perhaps Beryl intended to visit him. But a one-way ticket? If she was intending to move to London to be near Steve, then their relationship was much more significant than Amy seemed to realize.

Alone in her room again, she took out the ticket and examined it. She noticed it had apparently been purchased in London, so it seemed unlikely that Beryl had bought it herself. Had Steve bought it and sent it to her? She needed to talk to Winnie, Elizabeth decided, but since there was no telephone in Winnie's house, it would have to wait until tomorrow. She was much too weary to go out again tonight.

Detective work, she was beginning to discover, could be extremely tiring. And horribly frustrating. It seemed the more she learned, the more puzzling the entire business became. All that information kept buzzing around in her head, and none of it seemed to mean anything at all. If she had any sense she would just give up and hand everything over to the police. If it wasn't for Winnie and the poor woman's unshakable faith in her, that's exactly what she would do.

"You going out again tonight?" Edna Barnett hung the wet dishtowel over the edge of the gas stove to dry, then wiped her hands on her apron. "And what's that horrible smell?"

"It's flipping good pong," Polly said defensively. "I got it in Woolworth's. It's called Seven Eleven. What's the matter with it?" She stood in front of the mirror in the hallway and smeared bright red lipstick over her mouth. After rolling her lips together to get the color even, she studied herself critically in the mirror.

"I hope you're not chasing after those Yanks," Edna said, sounding cross. "You're too young to be mixed up with the likes of them. Too quick with their hands, they are."

Polly gave her mother a sly look. "How'd you know that, Ma?"

"Rita Crumm told me." Edna dumped the saucepans down on their shelf in the cupboard.

"Rita Crumm?" Polly let out a shout of laughter. "You telling me that Rita Crumm is running around with Yanks? She's old enough to be their flipping mother. Besides, she's married. What's Bert going to say when he hears about it?"

"For God's sake, Polly, I didn't say Rita was going after the Yanks. She was talking about Lilly."

Polly made a face at herself in the mirror. "Lilly gets what she deserves, running around in those tight jumpers, showing off what she's got. But then, what can you expect with a ma like Rita Crumm?"

"You watch your tongue, my girl. You were taught to respect your elders."

Marlene clattered down the stairs just then, almost toppling over on her high heels. Grabbing the handrail to steady herself, she pulled her shoe back on. "You nearly ready, then, Polly?"

"Yeah." Polly scrutinized herself one last moment in the mirror, then snatched up her handbag. "Ma was just telling me I should respect Rita Crumm."

Marlene's incredulous laugh sounded more like a snort. "You should go down the Tudor Arms one night, Ma, and watch Rita in action. She could teach us a thing or two, I can tell you."

"I should certainly hope so. She's a lot older than you are. And I hope I never catch either of you hanging around that pub." Red-faced, Edna reached for the scouring pad and began scrubbing the sink. "Just make sure that you keep Polly out of trouble, that's all I ask. I'm holding you responsible for your sister, Marlene. You hear me?"

"Ma," Marlene wailed, "I told you, Polly's a big girl. She can take care of herself."

Polly nodded vigorously. "Yeah, Ma, I'm a big girl. You don't have to worry about me. Come on, Marl."

Before her mother could answer, Polly had dragged her sister out of the house and slammed the door.

"She'd have a bloomin' fit if she knew we were going to the Tudor Arms to meet Yanks," Marlene said as the two of them set out down the road.

"What she don't know won't bother her." Polly shivered as the cool breeze brushed her bare arms. Having spent all her clothing coupons, she'd cut the sleeves off one of her blouses to make it look different. The armholes were a lot bigger than on a proper sleeveless blouse and let in more of the evening air than was comfortable. She had to keep her arms pressed to her sides so that no one would see her brassiere. Luckily Ma had been too busy with the washing up to notice. If she had, she'd have made her change into something else.

"I never used to mind this long walk to the pub," Marlene said, as their heels clicked loudly on the rough pavement of the country lane. "But ever since Beryl was murdered, I feel funny about walking along here at night. What if the murderer's still lurking about, looking for someone else to kill?"

Polly shivered again, though not from the sea breeze this time. "Get on with you, Marl. The murderer won't come down here. Too many people about. Beryl was killed on the coast road. Besides, it's not dark yet. Murderers don't usually kill people in daylight. They wait until it's dark."

"I bloody hope so." Marlene halted. "Listen, is that a lorry coming?"

Polly stopped, too, and turned around to face the lane they'd just come down. "Could be a jeep. Hope it is. If they're Yanks, we can ask them for a lift." The words were barely out of her mouth before an army jeep came careening around the corner on the wrong side of the road.

With a yelp both girls leapt for the ditch. The jeep barely missed them, then screeched to a halt in a cloud of dust.

"Gee, sorry, ma'am," a voice called out.

Seated side by side in the damp ditch, Polly and Marlene looked at each other. "Yanks," they both said together.

A tall, lanky GI appeared at the edge of the road, looking anxiously down at them. "You okay? Are you hurt?"

"Just our bloody pride," Marlene muttered. She picked herself up, then accepted the hand of the Yank, who hauled her out onto the road.

Polly waited until she was sure she had his attention then, as gracefully as she could manage, climbed to her feet. His fingers were warm and strong around hers as he pulled her out, and she felt the thrill right down to her bones. She was so enthralled she forgot all about her wide armholes.

Now that she could see the Yank better, she realized he was older than she first thought. He wore the uniform of a squadron leader or something, and he had gorgeous brown eyes and thick, dark hair. He was much better-looking than anyone she'd ever met in her life.

Still clinging to his hand, she tried to sound grown-up and seductive like the film stars when she murmured, "Hello, there. My name's Polly. This is my sister, Marlene."

Her voice had come out wrong. She'd sounded as if she had a bad cold. Marlene looked at her as if she'd said something daft, and Polly cleared her throat in embarrassment.

"Sam," the Yank said, giving her a grin that totally took her breath away. "Where are you girls going? Need a ride?"

Polly glanced at the jeep and for the first time noticed another GI behind the wheel. "We're going to the Tudor Arms," she said, finally letting go of Sam's hand. "And we'd love a lift, wouldn't we, Marl."

Marlene took a good look at the driver of the jeep. "That's very kind of you, I'm sure," she said, and started walking toward him.

"It's the least we can do," Sam said, taking Polly by the arm, "after almost running you down. We still can't get the hang of driving on the other side of the road."

She loved his voice, Polly thought dreamily. What a lovely accent. He sounded like a film star. He looked like a film star. All told, he was a right smasher. Just wait until she walked into the Tudor Arms with *him*. Every girl in the place would be drooling. She just hoped Lilly Crumm was in there. She'd show her she wasn't the only one who could get a Yank.

Sam introduced his friend, Clay, who wasn't as good-looking as Sam, but he had nice eyes. "You two old enough to drink?" he asked as Polly settled herself in the back next to Marlene.

"Course we are," Polly answered promptly. "Marlene's

eighteen and I'm—" She couldn't possibly tell him how old she really was. He'd think she was too young for him. He had to be at least twenty-four, maybe older. "I'm twenty," she said boldly.

Marlene made a small, strangled sound in the back of her throat.

Sam twisted his head around. "Twenty? You sure don't look it."

"That's what our ma's always saying, isn't she, Marl?" Polly nudged Marlene in the side. "She's always saying as how Marlene looks older than me, when it's the other way round."

The engine roared as the jeep took off. Both girls were jerked backward. They clung to the sides and screamed in unison, "Wrong side of the road!"

"Oh, shit." Clay swung the wheel over, and the vehicle leapt to the other side of the lane, rocking on two wheels.

"So, where do you two work?" Sam asked, when things had calmed down again.

"I'm a hairdresser," Marlene said, patting her ruffled red curls.

"Hey, how about that!" Sam nudged Clay hard in the arm, sending the jeep bouncing across the lane and back again. "We might get a free haircut if we're lucky."

You might get a lot more than that, Polly thought daringly. She was beginning to feel like a film star herself, doing exciting things in exciting company and living dangerously for once. Nothing like this had ever happened to her before. All the Yanks she'd spoken to up until now had been young and silly. All they wanted was to get a girl behind a barn. They had no class, no polish. Not like Sam. He was a real man. There was no doubt about it. For the first time in her life, she was in love.

She closed her eyes and imagined herself living with

Sam in Hollywood. She'd have a beautiful house with a swimming pool, and she'd drive a big red car, like in the films. She'd have beautiful clothes and servants . . .

"What about you, Polly?" Sam asked, breaking into her dream. "What do you do?"

She couldn't tell him she was a maid at the Manor House. She just couldn't. She searched her mind for something glamorous, while Marlene stared at her with the same look Ma got on her face when they got home late. "I'm a secretary," she said at last.

"Secretary," Sam repeated, sounding impressed. "Wow. So who do you work for, then?"

Polly pulled in a breath of fresh sea air. "I'm secretary to Lady Elizabeth Hartleigh Compton, up at the Manor House."

"No kidding!" Sam swiveled around in his seat to look at her. "Then I reckon we'll be seeing a lot of each other. I'm moving into quarters at the Manor House next week."

Speechless for once, Polly could only stare at him.

"Now you've done it," Marlene muttered. "Get yourself out of this one."

CHAPTER

❦ 11 ❦

Winnie seemed a little less overwrought when Elizabeth arrived at the house the next morning. "Lady Elizabeth! Any news?" she asked eagerly the second she opened the door.

"I do actually, but I'm not sure it helps all that much." Elizabeth followed her into the familiar parlor. "Though I have an appointment at the Land Army recruitment center this afternoon. I'm hoping the woman there can tell me something useful. And I talked to Amy." She accepted the cup of tea Winnie handed her and sat down on the sofa, which was strewn with clothes.

"I was just going through Beryl's things," Winnie said, gathering up the garments. "Thought I'd give them to the Red Cross. Help those poor people bombed out of their homes."

"That's very thoughtful." Elizabeth paused. "Maybe you should hang onto them for just a little while longer.

Until the person who killed your daughter has been apprehended. Just in case there's something we might have missed."

"Oh, right." Winnie looked depressed again. "I didn't think about that. I just wanted to get it over with, that's all."

"I can understand that." Elizabeth took a sip of the hot tea. "Have you heard from Stan?"

"Not a word. I've got no idea when he'll turn up."

"Yes, well, these things take time, I suppose." Elizabeth put her cup down carefully in the saucer. "Winnie, did Beryl ever mention a soldier by the name of Steve?"

Winnie wrinkled her brow. "Not that I remember. Why? Is he the one who gave her the badge?"

"I think he might be. Amy said he was stationed in London. I think he's the one who sent her the train ticket."

"I thought she bought that herself."

"No, unless she went to London to buy it." Elizabeth took the train ticket out of her purse. "If you look at it, you'll see it was purchased in London, two weeks ago."

"Well, I never. I never noticed that."

"Neither did I until last night," Elizabeth admitted. It wasn't often she felt unsure of herself, but this was the first time she'd been involved in anything as serious as murder. "I'm not terribly good at this detective thing," she admitted. "Perhaps it might be better if we give everything to George and Sid and let them sort it all out."

"Not on your life." Winnie got up and poured herself another cup of tea. "They'd make a blooming mess of it. They'd never have bothered talking to Amy, for a start." She came back to the table. "So, was it Amy who told you about this Steve, then?"

"Yes, she told me Beryl had been writing to him."

"Hmm. Beryl did get some letters from London, but she said they were from a girlfriend of hers who moved up there. Little cow. It looks as if she'd been lying to me all along, doesn't it." She broke off and pressed a hand to her lips, tears welling in her eyes.

Elizabeth waited, at a loss for words for once.

"I'm sorry, m'm. Just keeps coming over me. I'll be all right in a minute. If only her father hadn't had to go away, I swear none of this would have happened. She never did listen to me. Our Stan knew how to handle her. Put the fear of God in her, he did."

"You mustn't blame yourself, Winnie," Elizabeth said firmly. "This could well have happened even if Stan had been here. The war does strange things to people."

"And brings strange people to town," Winnie said darkly. "I don't know about this Steve person, but I wouldn't mind betting that one of them Yanks is at the bottom of this."

Elizabeth thought about the red circle on the map. She was reluctant to mention anything about it to Winnie. There was no point in getting her all stirred up about something until she knew more herself. And she wasn't going to know more if Major Monroe refused to help her.

"Do you have the letters Beryl got from London?" she asked, relieved to see that Winnie seemed to have collected herself again.

The other woman lifted her hands in a helpless gesture. "They're nowhere around here, or I would have seen them. And they're not in her room. You searched it yourself."

"Yes, I did." That brought up an interesting point. Apparently Beryl had either destroyed the letters or hidden them outside of the house. Yet Robbie's note had been tucked inside her pillow, as if she couldn't bear to part with it. That would seem as though Robbie's note meant more to Beryl than Steve's letters. If that were so, why would she plan to leave home to be with Steve? It didn't make sense. Right then, nothing at all made sense.

"I wonder what she did with them," Winnie said thoughtfully. "She must have thrown them away, but—" She broke off as the loud rap of the door knocker echoed from the front door. "Now who can that be? Excuse me, m'm. I won't be a minute."

She left the parlor, and Elizabeth heard her muffled exclamation, then George's booming voice. Apparently she invited him in, as a moment later Elizabeth heard him inside the sitting room. She didn't hear what he said, but she heard Winnie cry out, and she rose swiftly from her chair. Whatever it was, it had been a shock to Winnie. Surely something hadn't happened to Stan?

Unable to contain herself, she hurried out into the sitting room. Winnie sat on an armchair, rocking herself back and forth, both hands pressed to her mouth. George's face looked even more ruddy than usual as he nodded at Elizabeth. "Good morning, Lady Elizabeth. Pardon me for intruding, but I thought Winnie should know right away."

"Know what right away? What is it, George? Is it Stan?"

George sent a wary glance at Winnie, who lowered her hands and burst into tears. "Oh, Lady Elizabeth, you'll never guess what. Our Beryl was . . . having a baby."

"A baby?" Elizabeth whirled on George. "Is this true?"

"Yes, m'm." George cleared his throat and looked up at the ceiling. "The medical examiner just told me a little while ago. Beryl Pierce was at least two months along."

Elizabeth stared at him. This latest development brought

up some very interesting questions, the most important of which was the identity of the father. Was it Evan, Steve, or the elusive Robbie? Even more significant, could this pregnancy be the reason Beryl was killed? Now it was even more important that she track down Steve and Robbie. Somehow she had to find a way to persuade Major Monroe to cooperate with her—a task that seemed as distasteful as it was formidable.

George finally left after promising to let Winnie know if there were any further developments in the case. The second the door closed behind him, Winnie burst out, "I knew that Evan was up to no good with our Beryl. I just knew it. I told her she was too young to tie herself down to one boyfriend, but she wouldn't listen to me. No, not her. Knew it all, she did."

"Winnie," Elizabeth said gently, "we don't know for certain that it's Evan's baby."

Winnie's head shot up. "He's the only one she knew well enough to do *that* with, that's for sure."

Desperately trying to tread delicately, Elizabeth sat down next to the distraught woman. "Winnie, Beryl apparently knew Steve well enough to plan on moving to London."

"I suppose so."

"And what about the note from Robbie? They weren't exactly strangers, were they?"

Winnie gulped. "Oh, my Lord. What if it was someone else, and Evan found out she was having someone else's baby? He's got a jealous streak, that boy. I wouldn't put it past him to have throttled her."

Elizabeth shook her head. "I don't think it was Evan, Winnie."

"How can you be sure?"

"Because Beryl was alive on Sunday morning. You

said yourself that you heard her come in that night and that her bed had been slept in."

"Yes, I did, but—"

"Evan never left the house after he got home Saturday night, except to work with his father in the fields. His mother was quite definite about that."

Winnie looked unconvinced. "Maybe she's lying, m'm. Wouldn't put it past her. After all, Evan's the only one they got left at home. The other two are in the army. I'd do the same thing myself if it was me."

"I might have agreed with you," Elizabeth said slowly, "if it wasn't for one thing."

"What's that?"

"When Mrs. Potter told me that Evan never left the farm, we didn't even know at that point that Beryl was dead. It was assumed that Beryl simply hadn't turned up for a date. Daphne Potter would have had no reason to lie."

Winnie looked as if all the stuffing had been knocked out of her. "You're right, m'm. I hadn't thought of that."

"No, I think we must look elsewhere for our killer." Elizabeth rose to her feet, doing her best to sound more confident than she felt. "I do think I'll have a word with Evan, though. He might be more forthcoming in light of this news."

Winnie looked hopeful. "You think he knows something he doesn't want to tell you?"

Elizabeth sighed. "I think there are a lot of people around here who know more than they are willing to tell. The trick is to find a way to get them to talk."

"You'll do it, I know you will." Winnie got up and headed for the front door. "I have the utmost confidence in you, m'm. As everyone around here's always saying, once Lady Elizabeth makes up her mind to do something, the devil himself couldn't stop her."

"I'm very much afraid," Elizabeth murmured as she took her leave, "that this time I might very well be up against the devil himself. Or someone close to him."

Upon arriving at the Potter farm, she was greeted by Daphne Potter, who opened the door to her. Obviously surprised to see her, the farmer's wife invited her in and offered her a cup of tea.

"Thank you," Elizabeth said, giving the woman her most charming smile, "but actually I came to see Evan. I'd like to have a word with him."

"He's out in the wheat fields," Daphne Potter said, nodding at the window. "Been hard at it since dawn. I'm worried about him, to tell you the truth. He's been moping about ever since last weekend. Losing Beryl like that has hurt him dreadfully. He never hangs around the house as a rule. He and Jim don't get on very well. They've been at each other's throats ever since Timmy and Billy went off to war."

"Oh, I'm sorry to hear that," Elizabeth murmured.

"Yes, well, I think Evan feels as if he let his dad down. You know, not getting in the army like his brothers. Anyway, ever since then, he's been staying out of his way, spending most of his time in the Tudor Arms. Only now he hasn't been down there since Saturday night. Hasn't been anywhere, poor lamb. I told him this morning he should go down the pub for a pint, thinking it might cheer him up a bit, but he said he didn't feel like going anywhere without Beryl."

"That is sad," Elizabeth agreed. "I would like a word with him, if that's all right?"

"Of course, m'm. He's out there in the east field.

You'll find it easier if you go down the lane to the second gate."

Reaching the fields a few moments later, Elizabeth spotted Evan gathering the stacks of wheat that had already been cut, tied, and propped on end. She leaned her motorcycle next to the fence and opened the gate to let herself into the field.

Evan's horse and wagon were at the far side, and although she did her best to tread in between the rows of shorn wheat as she made her way across, the stubbly stalks scratched her ankles quite painfully, and she was limping when she finally reached Evan.

He paused in the act of swinging a pitchfork into the next stack of wheat and stared at her in astonishment when he caught sight of her. "Lady Elizabeth?" His glance slid past her, as if he half expected someone to be accompanying her. "What are you doing out here?" He snatched off his cap. "Begging your pardon, m'm. I just wasn't expecting you, that's all."

Elizabeth smiled. "I didn't mean to startle you, Evan. I just wanted to ask you if you knew . . . that Beryl was pregnant."

She'd hoped to shock him into a reaction, but he merely turned away from her and jabbed his pitchfork into the wheat. Lifting the heavy load with remarkable ease, he swung it onto the cart. "So I heard," he muttered at last. "P.C. Dalrymple already told me."

"I suppose you realize that people will think you are the father."

Evan's face turned bright red. Eyes blazing, he jabbed the pitchfork into the wheat with such force it toppled over. "I ain't the bleeding father," he said with a belligerence that surprised Elizabeth. "I told the constable that. Me and Beryl never went that far. She would never let me. I didn't even know she was in the family way. Never bloody told me about it."

There was a ring of credibility in his voice, and something else—a tinge of disbelief—that convinced Elizabeth he was telling the truth. Obviously the news of Beryl's condition had come as a shock to the young man.

Feeling sorry for him, Elizabeth said quietly, "Are you sure there isn't anything you can tell me that might help discover who was responsible for Beryl's condition?"

"No, m'm. Nothing." He grabbed the pitchfork and swung the stack up onto the wagon. "Beryl's always been secretive, if you know what I mean. She changed a lot since her dad went off in the navy. Started wearing cheap clothes, had her hair cut off, plastered her face with makeup. I hardly knew her anymore. I told her she was looking common, but she wouldn't listen to me. I told her she'd end up in trouble, going around looking like that . . ." His voice trailed off, and he leaned his shoulder against the wagon, obviously fighting genuine emotion.

"Well, thank you, Evan. I'm sorry I upset you." Elizabeth left him to his grief and trudged back across the field to her motorcycle. She felt as sure as she could be that Evan was not the father of Beryl's baby. That left Steve . . . or Robbie. Maybe Carol Simmons, the woman in the recruitment center, could tell her something that might help.

Mindful of her disguise as an applicant for the Land Army, she dressed carefully for her visit to North Horsham. She'd found a sensible white cotton skirt to wear, wide enough to give her the room she needed on her motorcycle. Thanks to the shortage of fabrics, most of the new clothes nowadays were so narrow she found it impossible to sit astride the saddle, and one could hardly ride a motorcycle sidesaddle like a horse.

Her pink jumper had been knitted by Violet, in the days when one could still buy enough wool to make a sweater. She simply could not go out without a hat, and after much dithering among her abundant choices finally settled on a black beret set jauntily at an angle and secured with a butterfly hatpin.

Feeling somewhat dowdy in the simple clothes, Elizabeth roared down the main street of North Horsham, collecting curious stares from those who were not familiar with the late Earl of Wellsborough's daughter and were no doubt wondering why such a fragile-looking woman would use such a precarious mode of transportation.

Which just went to show, Elizabeth thought, not without some satisfaction, that they didn't know her at all. People, even ones she knew, sometimes underestimated her strengths. What she lacked in muscle she made up for in determination. Where there was a will, there was a way, as the saying went. And Lady Elizabeth Hartleigh Compton had quite a formidable will.

It held her in good stead when she marched into the recruitment center and asked for Carol Simmons. The stern-looking woman behind the counter didn't even look up. "You need to fill out an application first."

"I beg your pardon?"

"You don't see Carol until you fill out an application."

Interesting, Elizabeth thought, since Beryl's application wasn't filled out. Maybe Carol Simmons would be helpful after all. She sat down at a small card table to fill out the form, using a fictitious address. Once she had gained Carol Simmons's confidence, she decided, she could simply say she'd changed her mind about joining the Land Army.

When she had answered all the questions, she laid the

form down in front of the surly woman, who waved a hand at a door across the room. "Take it with you. In there."

"Thank you, you're so terribly kind." Ignoring the woman's startled expression, Elizabeth crossed the room and tapped gently on the door before opening it.

A young woman sat at a small desk littered with papers. "Come in and sit down," she said, also without bothering to look up. She seemed to be engrossed in the sheet of paper in her hand.

Elizabeth laid the application form on the desk and sat down on a very uncomfortable slatted chair.

After several irritating moments of silence broken only by the scratching of Carol Simmons's pen, the woman finally reached for the form and drew it toward her. "Ms. Compton," she said, studying the sheet of paper, "have you had any experience with farm work?"

Elizabeth thought about it. "I've ridden a few horses in my time."

Carol Simmons got a look on her face that clearly showed her exasperation. "No experience." She scribbled something on the form. "I suppose it's too much to expect you know how to drive a tractor. How about a motorcar?"

"Actually I ride a motorcycle," Elizabeth said, beginning to feel somewhat inadequate.

That raised the other woman's head. "A motorcycle?" She stared at Elizabeth for a moment, then narrowed her eyes. "Wait a minute. Don't I know you? I've seen you somewhere before . . ."

Elizabeth's heart sank. She wished now she hadn't given in to the silly impulse to hide her identity. She was taking this detective business far too seriously. If she wasn't careful, she warned herself, she could very easily get herself into serious trouble. And judging from the way Carol Simmons was glaring at her, that trouble could very well be about to descend on her head.

CHAPTER
❈ 12 ❈

In a last-ditch attempt to bluff her way out, Elizabeth shook her head. "I don't think—"

"Yes, I've got it." Carol Simmons snapped her fingers. "You're Lady Elizabeth something or other. From the manor at Sitting Marsh. I saw your picture in the papers, giving a speech at the flower show."

"Well, now that you mention it—"

"Here! You've been giving me a bunch of lies." Carol Simmons surged from her seat. She was a very large lady, with arms the size of tree trunks.

Looking at the fierce scowl on her face, Elizabeth decided it might not be prudent to attempt to deceive her any further. "Miss Simmons—"

"You lied to me. You're not here to join the Land Army. I could have you arrested. How do I know you're not in here to steal government secrets?"

Elizabeth's temper finally came to the rescue. "Young

lady!" Her voice snapped across the room with the sting of a whiplash. "I have no interest whatsoever in your precious government secrets. Furthermore, I am not accustomed to being addressed in that vulgar manner. I regret my small deception, but under the circumstances, I felt you might feel too constricted to talk freely if you were aware of my true identity. Obviously I needn't have worried. You apparently have no concept of polite conversation with a member of gentility."

Carol Simmons opened her mouth, shut it again, and slumped down on her chair. "Well, excuse me, your ladyship," she muttered. "But I have to be careful these days. For all I know, you could have been a spy."

"And you could easily be Mussolini in disguise." Elizabeth crossed her arms. "I am, however, prepared to give you the benefit of the doubt. I'd appreciate it if you would offer the same courtesy."

She immediately. regretted her vulgar outburst, but Carol Simmons apparently had thick skin. She merely shrugged. "I'm just trying to do my job. So what did you come here for, if you didn't come to join the Land Army . . . your ladyship?"

Elizabeth wisely ignored the tinge of sarcasm. "I wanted to ask you about someone I believe might have been a friend of yours." She opened her handbag and took out the application form then passed it across the desk, the smudged side uppermost. "Is this your handwriting?"

Carol Simmons stared at the telephone number for a moment. "Yes, it is. Where did you get this?" She looked up sharply. "It was you on the telephone yesterday, wasn't it? The friend of Beryl Pierce?"

"Yes." Elizabeth nodded at the sheet of paper in Carol

Simmons's hand. "That paper was discovered in the saddlebag of Beryl's bicycle."

The other woman frowned. "Beryl? But I don't understand. I—"

"Miss Simmons, I don't know if you have heard the sad news, but Beryl was killed last Saturday. I'm sorry if she was a friend of yours—"

She broke off as Carol uttered a sharp cry. "Killed? How?"

"We don't know that yet. The police are working on the case at the moment." Anticipating the next question, she added hurriedly, "I offered to assist the police by asking some of Beryl's friends if they knew anything that could help in the investigation."

Carol's face had gone quite white. "I didn't know her very well," she said faintly. "I . . . we met at a dance in North Horsham. She asked me about the Land Army, and I wrote down my number on the back of a form to give her. That was the last time I saw her. I swear."

"Then you wouldn't know any of Beryl's boyfriends."

It seemed as if the answer came a little too fast. "No, m'm. None at all. Sorry I can't help you."

"Did you happen to see her with anyone at the dance?"

Carol Simmons shrugged, though the expression on her face was far from casual. "I saw her with lots of people at the dance. But I couldn't tell if any of them were her boyfriend. She was throwing herself at everyone who looked at her, if you know what I mean." The bitter note in her voice clearly conveyed her disapproval.

Elizabeth took back the form and tucked it into her handbag again. "Well, I'm sorry to have taken up your time, Miss Simmons. Thank you for answering my questions."

"I'm sorry I couldn't be more help." Carol Simmons

picked up a pencil and started tapping it on the desk. "Perhaps you could let me know if they find out who did it?"

"I'm sure when they do the news will be all over the newspapers." Elizabeth reached the door and looked back. "I'm surprised an account of Beryl's death isn't in it already."

"Well, it's the war, I expect. Papers are full of it these days. Don't have room for nothing else."

"Quite." Elizabeth nodded, then let herself out into the noisy street. A double-decker bus roared by, sending black smoke and fumes into the sunny afternoon. She couldn't wait to get back to the peace and quiet of Sitting Marsh, especially since her trip here appeared to be in vain. Though something told her that Carol Simmons wasn't telling her everything she knew. She couldn't help wondering just what it was the woman was trying to hide.

On her way back to the village, Elizabeth decided to take a look at the area where Beryl's bicycle was found. She couldn't imagine what she might find, since both George and Sid had thoroughly searched the area, according to them. Still, in all the mysteries she'd read, the detective always examined the scene of the crime, and so far she hadn't done that yet.

She smiled to herself as she sailed down the coast road to the cliffs. In spite of the hazards, she rather liked thinking of herself as a detective. Sort of exciting, really. Although a lot of times her efforts ended in frustration, it did give her a sense of achievement when another piece of the puzzle surfaced. She'd always enjoyed working with a jigsaw puzzle, and trying to solve a murder was somewhat similar. Except that right now she had lots of pieces of the puzzle, and none of them fit in anywhere. To make matters worse, something kept niggling in the back of her mind: a feeling that she'd missed something important, though she couldn't imagine what it might be.

She was still wrestling with the problem when she rounded the curve and almost ran into a large group of women, all of whom apparently had a death wish, since they were strung across the road elbow to elbow. After frantically applying the brakes and narrowly avoiding a nasty skid, Elizabeth was further unnerved by the sight of each woman holding a pitchfork, a garden spade, or some other equally threatening weapon in her hand.

"Halt!" The lanky woman in the middle stepped forward and held up a commanding hand. "Who goes there?"

With a sinking feeling in the pit of her stomach, Elizabeth recognized Rita Crumm, a woman notorious for her penchant for ferreting out the tiniest whisper of gossip and repeating it loudly enough and often enough for the entire community to hear. Usually with some kind of embellishment to render her news even more interesting.

Elizabeth shut off her engine, which had the immediate effect of silencing the excited gabbling of the women.

"Stand forward and be recognized!" Rita Crumm demanded.

Someone in the crowd tittered and earned a ferocious glare from her leader.

Obviously, Elizabeth thought sourly, Rita had seen the main attraction at the Odeon last week—an epic about the Foreign Legion, according to Polly. Elizabeth had overheard her discussing the film with Violet.

"It's Lady Elizabeth, Rita," a timid voice offered, stating the obvious, while a faint chorus of polite greetings echoed her announcement.

Since Rita could hardly continue refusing to recognize her, Elizabeth saw no reason to obey the ridiculous command. Instead, she straightened her beret, which had dislodged itself during her abrupt halt and was sitting sideways over her ear.

Uncomfortably aware of her unusually drab attire, she viewed Rita and her consorts with the same expression she might use had she met with a dead rat on the road. "May I ask what in the world you are all doing? Other than embarking on a suicide mission, that is. Have you forgotten that the Americans constantly use this road, and that they have absolutely no concept of the correct side on which to drive their lorries?"

The women nudged each other, accompanied by a ripple of loud muttering down the line. Rita's face turned a deep shade of purple, and she threw a fierce glare over her shoulder at the more audible members of her entourage. "Quiet!" She was a tall, thin woman—taller than most, and her imperious, sergeant-major voice had a note of authority that once more silenced her unruly followers.

Turning back to face front, Rita drew herself up to her full height, which was quite impressive, as even Elizabeth had to admit. "Excuse me, Lady Elizabeth, but we happen to be in training for a very important event. I have to ask you to identify yourself. It's part of the procedure."

"In training? For what?"

"The invasion, m'm. We have to be prepared. Now that all the able-bodied men have gone, it's us women who will have to fight the Germans when they land."

"Are we about to be invaded? I haven't heard anything on the wireless." With a spasm of trepidation Elizabeth scanned the motley line of would-be warriors. Most of them looked as if they couldn't take more than a few steps without running out of breath. Really, it was quite amazing how rotund these housewives could look, in view of the rationing. If there were, indeed, an invasion from the Germans, and these women were the only barrier standing between them and the villagers of Sitting Marsh, there didn't seem to be a whole lot of hope for their future.

"They might not actually be on the way, Lady Elizabeth, but as long as them bloody Nazis . . . begging your pardon, m'm, but as long as them Nazis are sitting right there on the beaches of France and Belgium, there's a chance they could sneak across and take us by surprise. We always have to be on guard. That's what my little army is here for—to keep our village safe from those murderers."

Elizabeth nodded, feeling somewhat relieved. Apparently this was more a case of Rita Crumm relieving her boredom with another of her outrageous displays than an imminent threat from the hapless Germans. Rita was renowned for organizing the villagers into doing something spectacular and, more often than not, disastrous.

Where most of the women were content with growing extra vegetables in their gardens, knitting scarves and gloves for the men in the trenches, or collecting pots and pans and tinfoil for the airplane factories, Rita's idea of a war effort was to stage a full-blown extravaganza designed to grab the attention of the entire village and surrounding areas, thus establishing herself as a sort of modern-day Joan of Arc, smiting a blow for the Allies. At least, that was Rita's intention, by her own proud admission.

Although Elizabeth hated to admit it, she was often goaded into competition with the woman, not because she craved attention and glory but simply because she felt a need to establish the line of authority in Sitting Marsh. Left to her own devices, Rita Crumm was quite capable of destroying the entire community with her misguided enthusiasm, and Elizabeth felt compelled to demonstrate the true source of leadership. Which was, after all, handed down from generation to generation by her worthy ancestors.

That wasn't always easy in this modern world, and especially in these uncertain times. In fact, Elizabeth had suffered more than one disaster herself in her efforts to maintain superiority over her rival.

"Well, I admire your vigilance," she told Rita, who was apparently waiting for some kind of rapturous praise for her brilliance. "I feel compelled to point out, however, that taking up this position on a blind curve is placing your little army in danger of being mowed down, if not by the Americans, then at least by a motorcar, which will render your troops somewhat ineffective should the Germans decide to visit us."

Rita's bony nose twitched. "This spot, Lady Elizabeth, is the best place for viewing the entire beach. You can see right down the coast from here. We should be able to spot a U-boat the minute it pops its ugly head up out of the sea. We don't want those buggers creeping up on us and taking us by surprise, now do we?"

"I'm sure we'll be somewhat forewarned." Elizabeth waved a hand at the cliffs and their thick necklace of barbed wire. "I can't imagine that an army of soldiers can cross the sands without stepping on at least one mine. In any case, I rather think they'll wait until nightfall to creep ashore, wouldn't you say?"

"We can't come out at night, Lady Elizabeth," one of the women piped up. "We have to take care of the children. We can only do this while they're at school."

"Ladies! We'd have to come out here no matter when the Germans get here." Rita turned on the unlucky protestor, apparently sensing a loss of the upper hand. "We all have to fight. Every last one of us. If any one of you hears those church bells ringing the alarm in the middle of the night, you wake everybody up, children and all, and get out here as fast as you can. That's the whole point of us training now, so we all know what to do when the Germans get here. We have to stop them somehow."

Rita threw her arm dramatically across her chest to smite it, a little too hard apparently, since she spluttered and coughed. Her next words, no doubt intended to be delivered in ringing tones, came out in more of a strangled croak. "It's your duty to God and your country."

The women looked at each other, obviously losing their zeal for the operation with the prospect of a confrontation at night.

"I wouldn't want to come out here in the dark," one woman said, her voice quavering. "Look what happened to poor Beryl Pierce. Just riding along here on her bicycle, she was, when some horrible murderer jumped out and grabbed her."

There was a general muttering of agreement and apprehension from the crowd. "Strangled her, he did," another woman confirmed.

"Yeah, and tossed her broken body into the sea."

"Oo, heck," a young housewife moaned, "I'm scared to be here even in daylight."

"I wonder if it was the Germans?" The frazzled-looking speaker looked nervously at Rita. "They could have come and gone, and we never heard them."

A chorus of frightened moans greeted this theory.

"Of course they did. Silly, silly me." In a fury of frustration, Rita exploded. "The entire German army landed on our beach, climbed our cliffs, murdered our Beryl, and then, thoroughly satisfied with their night's work, crept back across a beach full of mines to their bloody submarine!" Her voice rose to a howl. "Why didn't I think of that?"

Her army, suitably impressed, gazed at her open-mouthed.

Elizabeth beamed, well pleased with the way things were turning out.

"Anyhow," someone said, "it wasn't the Germans. It was one of them bloody Yanks."

Her smile fading, Elizabeth jumped in to dispel the speculation before it got out of hand. "There is absolutely no reason to put the blame for Beryl's death on an American. It could have been anyone."

"More likely she was having some Yank's baby, and he got rid of it and her with it," Rita said with a little too much confidence for comfort.

"I think it would be a big mistake to spread rumors like that." Elizabeth appealed to the rest of the women. "We really don't want any trouble with the Americans, do we? It's really not fair to blame them for everything that goes wrong."

"Murdering one of our young girls is a lot more than something going wrong," Rita insisted. "Everyone knows what Beryl was—and she was as silly over the Yanks as the rest of the girls. I saw her myself, clinging to the arm of one of them, gazing up into his face as if he was Clark Gable."

"Oo, if he was Clark Gable, I'd be clinging and gazing at him meself," someone said.

Everyone laughed, breaking the tension. Elizabeth smiled with them, then amid a chorus of good-byes, fired up her engine and took off up the lane. Once out of sight, her smile disappeared. The problem was, Rita could well be right, especially if she was telling the truth about see-

ing Beryl with an American. And there was no reason
for Elizabeth to suspect otherwise. Rita might exaggerate
from time to time, but she'd never been known to deliberately make something up.

It seemed as if her suspicions were right, Elizabeth
thought, her mind going back once more to that small
red circle on the map. She couldn't ignore the possibility
any longer. She would have to ask Major Monroe to help
her. In any case, it would probably be only a matter of
time before George and Sid came to the same conclusion,
and she hated to think what trouble they could cause at
the base if they started poking around there.

She used that prospect to strengthen her case when she
finally got through to the major that evening. When she'd
first called she'd been told he was unavailable. Although
he obviously couldn't mention it, she guessed he'd been
on a mission with his men. He sounded unutterably
weary, as only a man can sound when he has looked
death in the face.

Her insides cringed in sympathy. She could only imagine what it must be like to take an airplane over enemy
territory, knowing full well the odds of coming back
alive.

He sounded surprised to hear from her. "I hope there
aren't any problems with us moving in next week?" he
asked as soon as he heard her voice.

"None at all." She paused, wondering how best to put
this. "Actually I called to ask you a favor. A big one,
I'm afraid, but I don't know what else to do." She re-
membered his words the last time she'd mentioned
Beryl's death. *This is a job for the police.* She could only
hope that he would prefer dealing with her rather than
two retired constables who had long ago lost their alacrity
for such a demanding job.

"Okay, shoot. If it's in my power, I'll be happy to do it."

"Well, it's rather delicate, to tell you the truth. You remember the map I showed you when you were at the house?"

There was a slight pause. "The map of the U.S. Yeah, I remember."

She heard the edge to his voice and crossed her fingers. "Well, I was looking at it later and I saw a small red circle drawn around a town called Camden, in New Jersey. Are you familiar with it?"

"Nope. Too far away from my neck of the woods."

"Well, that's why I was asking. I was wondering if it had any sort of significance. Other than being someone's hometown, I mean."

He caught on very fast. "Like the murdered girl's boyfriend. Is that what you're getting at?"

"Look, Major, I know this is awkward for you, and I don't blame you for being reluctant to discuss it with me. But if I don't find out what happened to Beryl soon, the constables will eventually form the same conclusions I have, and I'm afraid they can be rather bullheaded when it comes to an investigation. All I want you to do is to find out if there is someone stationed at your base by the name of Robbie who lives in a town called Camden, in New Jersey."

"And what if I find him? Technically he's on American territory. I can't allow you to question him, not without some kind of official order."

Elizabeth squeezed her crossed fingers tighter. "Yes, I'm aware of that. I was sort of hoping you could ask him a question or two."

A longer pause this time. "I could ask him, I reckon, but I can't force him to answer."

"No, I don't suppose you can." Elizabeth sighed. "Still, anything is better than nothing at all. He might be able to clear up a few things for me."

"Always supposing this guy exists."

"Yes, of course." She felt depressed. The major didn't sound as if he was prepared to make any special effort to get at the truth. She could hardly blame him. This wasn't his town or even his country. He was defending his men, as any good commanding officer would do in the face of adversity. Still, she had to make one last appeal to Earl Monroe's sense of justice.

"Major," she said carefully, "I should tell you that Beryl Pierce was having a baby. That could be the reason she was killed. I'm sure you are as anxious as I am to see that the person who was responsible for taking this young girl's life is punished in an appropriate manner."

He was silent for so long she thought they might have been cut off. Then his deep voice echoed in her ear. "I'll do my best to track him down. That's all I can promise right now."

Feeling only slightly better, she thanked him and hung up. She hoped and prayed he could find the man and clear him of the crime. She hated to think of the trouble it would cause in Sitting Marsh and probably as far as North Horsham, too, if Beryl's murderer turned out to be an American.

It wouldn't take very much for everyone to turn on them, especially the men. Already there had been fights in the Tudor Arms with soldiers of the British army. With most of the villagers up in arms about the problems and the prospect of housing the enemy in her home, so to speak, things could get very uncomfortable indeed.

CHAPTER

❦ 13 ❦

"I'm going to shoot that Desmond if he doesn't wipe his feet on the mat." Violet waved an arm at the muddy footprints marching across the tiled kitchen floor. "Just look at that mess. He should be made to come in and clean it up, filthy bugger. I bet he doesn't do that in his own home. Sheila would kill him."

Elizabeth nodded absently. Her mind was on more absorbing situations than a dirty kitchen floor. She kept thinking about Major Monroe and wondering if he'd keep his promise to find Beryl's Robbie.

"It wouldn't hurt him to clean up before he comes in my kitchen, neither. I don't think he even washes his hands."

"Perhaps not," Elizabeth murmured.

"I watched him this morning. He stood right here in the middle of the floor and took off all his clothes."

Violet's words finally penetrated. Elizabeth jerked up her chin. "What?"

"Just wanted to make sure you were listening." Violet walked over to the table and sat down. "What's wrong, Lizzie? You haven't been yourself lately. Not ill, are you?"

Elizabeth smiled and shook her head. She was at a loss to explain her occasional bouts of melancholy, but neither did she feel like discussing them. "It's such a lovely day," she said, glancing at the open bay window, where yellow curtains wafted gently in the breeze. "How I wish I could take a long walk on the beach. I miss that so much."

"So do I." Violet sighed. "I wonder if the sands will ever be the same again once this war is over. It seems years since we had visitors. We don't even get people on the Stately Homes Tour anymore."

"It has been a while," Elizabeth agreed. "Not many people go on day trips these days. Most men are serving in the forces, and women don't like to go out without them."

"Doesn't seem to bother the women around here," Violet said tartly. "From what I hear, the pubs are full of them."

"Well, it's just as well we don't get the tour people now that we'll have the Americans in the house. It would make things very awkward. We would have to close off the most interesting part of the house."

"Oh, I don't know." Violet gave her a wicked grin. "I'd say that visiting the east wing with the Americans there would make the tour even more exciting."

"Not for the Americans, I imagine." Elizabeth propped her chin on her hand. "Violet, what do you think about getting a dog?"

"A dog? Why would I want a dog? More mess to clear up, that's what I say."

"I was thinking of getting one or two for company." Becoming enthused by the idea, Elizabeth sat up. "Cocker spaniels, I think. Or maybe something bigger. Red setters?"

Violet frowned. "You're serious about this?"

"Yes, I am. I think it would be fun to have a couple of dogs about the house." She jumped up from her chair. "In fact, I think I'll take a ride out to Gridlington Corners. I know there are several breeders in that area. I can make a decision after I've talked to some of them."

Violet got up more slowly. "You don't think that having a houseful of Americans is enough excitement around here?"

Elizabeth patted her bony shoulder. "Don't worry about the dogs, Violet. I'll take care of them."

Violet rolled her eyes. "Where have I heard that before?"

"I'm a lot older now. This time I intend to take care of them myself."

"What about this murder investigation? Have you given up on that yet?"

Elizabeth paused at the door. "Not really. I'm waiting to hear from . . . someone who might be able to help in that."

Violet sent her one of her sharp looks. "Nothing that's going to get you in trouble, I hope. You've been running here and there a lot lately. I wouldn't want you to get into something you'll be sorry for later."

"I promise you, Violet, I'm not getting into any trouble. I'll be back in an hour or so." She couldn't help feeling guilty as she wheeled her motorcycle out of the stable. She had deliberately kept quiet about her activities the past day or two, knowing how much Violet would worry and fuss if she knew to what extent she was pursuing Beryl's killer.

She spent the morning touring the breeders' kennels, and by the time she left she still hadn't made up her mind which breed of dog she wanted. It was just too hard to concentrate, when all she had on her mind was how soon Major Monroe was going to let her know if he'd found Robbie.

When she returned to the Manor House, she had to ring the bell four times before Martin finally arrived at the door. Violet, apparently, was busy in the kitchen. One of these days, she promised herself, she would have a proper lock installed, one that she could open with a key, instead of the latches and bolts that secured the impressive entrance of the manor.

Now and again, if she was in a great hurry, she made her way around the house to the back door, but that meant tramping across the vegetable gardens and through the greenhouses, where she was invariably waylaid by Desmond, whose phlegmatic meanderings drove her absolutely potty.

Almost three minutes elapsed by the time Martin finally completed the complicated maneuver of opening the door, moving far enough back for her to step inside, then closing the door securely behind her.

Heaven help him if the Germans ever decided to drop their bombs on Sitting Marsh. Elizabeth wondered how her American visitors would react to this agonizing process of getting into the house. Military people expected everything to be done promptly and with the utmost speed. Uncle Roger, her father's brother, was a colonel in the Royal Fusiliers. She'd learned more about the British Army from him than any civilian should ever have to know.

Speed and alacrity, he was fond of telling his bored niece, was imperative. It could mean the difference between life and death. If the Americans were to rely on Martin for their survival, they'd be doomed.

"They came for the saucepans today, madam," Martin announced, just as Elizabeth headed for the stairs.

She paused in midstride. "The saucepans, Martin?"

"Yes, madam."

Elizabeth retraced her steps. "Who came for them?"

"I'm not quite sure, madam. I think it was the War Office."

"Did they give you a receipt?"

"I think Violet has one, yes, madam. She gave them the saucepans."

Elizabeth tapped her foot on the carpet. The government had already confiscated most of the iron railings and the ornamental gate that had once barred the entrance to the driveway. Now they were after the saucepans. True, the country was in dire need of heavy metals for the airplanes, but it was really quite frustrating to have to hand over one's precious personal household items.

"Which of the saucepans did Violet give them?" she asked him, hoping that her housekeeper had enough sense not to hand over the family heirlooms.

"The tin ones you told Violet to purchase from the gypsies last year." Martin glanced in the tiny, diamond-shaped mirror set into the hallstand and smoothed a hand over his three strands of hair. "Violet said they were inferior."

"So they were," Elizabeth agreed, much relieved. "I only bought them to give that poor woman some money. She looked half starved when she came to the door."

"Well, I certainly hope they warn the soldiers they are inferior before they use them. Though I really can't understand why they don't use helmets."

Elizabeth turned this over in her mind, hoping that the words would begin to make some sense. Finally giving up, she took a wild shot at it. "The soldiers won't be using the saucepans for cooking, Martin. And I doubt very much if they'd be allowed to cook in their helmets."

Martin looked startled. "Cook in their helmets, madam? I should say not."

There were times, Elizabeth thought, when she seriously considered the possibility that she was the one going senile. "Sorry, Martin. You're confusing me."

"If I may say so, madam, it is I who am confused. A soldier would never cook in his helmet. Unheard of, I should say."

"Quite." Totally baffled, which was not unusual when trying to follow Martin's train of thought, Elizabeth turned for the stairs again, and heard Martin muttering behind her.

"Soldiers cooking in their helmets. What nonsense. They should be wearing them on their heads instead of inferior saucepans. What sort of protection will saucepans provide in the heat of battle, I ask you?"

Elizabeth continued heading for the stairs. The best thing to do in these circumstances was completely ignore him. She just couldn't resist giving it one last shot, however. "The soldiers don't wear the saucepans for protection, Martin. People melt them down to make parts for airplanes."

She left Martin struggling with the logistics of that and retired to her room.

Major Monroe came to the house late that afternoon. Elizabeth, who was in the conservatory at the time reading the latest edition of *Film Parade*, heard his familiar voice as Violet led him into the adjoining library.

She hid the magazine under the bright blue cushion of her white wicker divan and waited for Violet to make her announcement.

A moment later Violet pushed open the door and stuck her head in. "Prince Charming's here," she hissed in a loud whisper.

Probably loud enough for the major to hear, Elizabeth thought, frowning at her. "You may show him in, Violet."

The housekeeper looked astounded. "In here?"

Elizabeth's frown intensified. "Yes, Violet. In here."

"If you say so." Violet withdrew her head. From inside the library, Elizabeth heard her say, "You can go in, Major."

Bracing herself, she wished she'd had time to run a comb through her hair, and at least put on a dab of lipstick. She rose as the major's tall figure appeared in the doorway. "Come in, Major Monroe. This is a surprise."

"Lady Elizabeth. I sure hope it's not an unpleasant surprise." He'd removed his cap and held it in his hand as he ventured into the narrow, fragrance-drenched room.

She saw his gaze drawn by the wide vista of gardens spreading beyond the conservatory and realized she was holding her breath. This small room, with its glass walls overlooking the grounds and its massive pots of tropical plants was her private haven. This was where she sought refuge when the pressures of her obligations and duties became too harrowing to bear.

She seldom entertained in this room. She wasn't entirely sure why she was doing so now. It was important to her, however, that Major Monroe approve of her sanctuary, now that he'd been given the privilege of visiting it.

He didn't disappoint her. "Magnificent view," he murmured. "This is a dandy room. Looking out at a scene like that, you can almost forget there's a war on."

"I often do." She smiled, pleased with his reaction. "Sit down, Major. I hope you have some news for me?"

He turned then to look at her, and his expression worried her. His resentment at being put in a difficult position was clearly written on his face. "Yes, ma'am. I do." He took the seat she offered him—a small, wicker rocking chair. "What's that smell? It seems vaguely familiar, but I can't place it."

"It's either the ginger plant you can smell or maybe hibiscus." She waved a hand at the colorful blooms in a bright corner of the room. "I have both."

He nodded. "That's where I've smelled that scent before. In Hawaii."

"You've been to Hawaii?" She stared at him in awe. "That's one place I've always wanted to see."

"Well, you wouldn't want to be there right now, ma'am."

Remembering the pictures she'd seen of the devastation of Pearl Harbor, she had to agree. "I suppose not. This dreadful war. It changes so many aspects of our lives."

"None more than right here, I reckon."

She shrugged. "We're lucky, really, being so far from the city. Apart from the inconveniences of rationing and shortages, the lack of manpower and the occasional enemy fighter pilot straying off course, we're rather far removed from the worst of it."

"That might change, now that the Americans are building and taking over air bases all over the country."

She looked at him in alarm. "You really think so?"

"Who knows? But if I were Hitler, I'd sure want to destroy as many enemy aircraft as humanly possible."

"Oh, lord. I hadn't thought of that. I suppose so. Poor Martin."

"Martin?"

"Our butler."

"You have a butler?"

"Yes, haven't you met him? A rather frail, elderly gentleman. Almost completely bald and wearing glasses. Dark suit and black bowtie."

"Oh, the old gentleman. I thought he was someone's uncle." He gave her a quizzical look. "He seems a little confused at times."

Elizabeth sighed. "Poor Martin. I'm afraid his duties have become a little too much for him. He does what he can, of course, and Violet and I sort of . . . fill in, I suppose you'd say."

"And you still keep him on?"

"He's been with the family since 1887. A little long to be put out to pasture, wouldn't you think?"

"Holy cow!" Earl Monroe's dark eyebrows shot up. "How old is he?"

"He'll be eighty-four in September. I believe he was twenty-nine when he first came to the Manor House. My father was one year old at the time."

"He's seen a few wars, then. Your butler, I mean."

"Yes, he has." Elizabeth sighed. "I only hope he survives this one." She stared at her clasped hands for a moment, wondering what she would do without Martin's bowed figure hovering about the house. He had been in her life forever. She would miss him a great deal.

Throwing off her sudden fit of despondency, she

smiled at the major. "Anyway, what have you come to tell me? You found Robbie?"

"Yes, ma'am. I did. His name is Corporal Robert Barrows. His hometown is Camden, New Jersey."

She curled her fingers into her palms. "And he told you he knew Beryl Pierce?"

"Yes, ma'am." The major stared down at his cap, which he still held in his hands, now twisting it around and around.

Guessing his thoughts, Elizabeth said quietly, "I can't promise anything, Major, but I'll do my very best to keep this information just between us. Unless Corporal Barrows admits to strangling Beryl. Then the British police will have a say in it, no doubt."

"He didn't kill her, ma'am."

The conviction in his voice impressed her. "You're quite certain of that?"

"As sure as I can be. Barrows never left the base the weekend she was killed. He was confined to quarters for causing a disturbance in the mess hall. There are several witnesses who can testify to that."

"I see." Elizabeth slumped in her chair. Another dead end. "Did he tell you anything about his association with Beryl?"

He flicked a glance at her. "Yes, ma'am, he did. But since he's not a suspect, I figure what he told me doesn't have to be a matter of record."

"You're quite right, of course. It doesn't." She sent him a look of appeal. "Whatever he told you, however, might help me. If I swear to keep whatever you tell me utterly confidential, would you consider sharing his comments with me?"

She waited, hardly daring to breathe, until finally the

major gave a curt nod of his head. "Very well, ma'am. I guess I'll have to trust you on that."

"Thank you, Major."

"I do have one question first."

"And what's that?"

"Why are you having so much trouble calling me Earl?"

Unsettled by the unexpected question, she thought about it before she answered. "I don't mean to be anti-social," she said finally. "I'm not aware of the customs in your country, but I think I can safely assume that they are a good deal more lax than those of the British Isles. A lady does not call a gentleman by his Christian name until she is very well acquainted with him."

His sharp gaze made her nervous. "I wouldn't want to violate any of your social customs, Lady Elizabeth, but it seems to me that in times of war like this one, if we waited to get to know someone before we felt at ease with him, that person might not be around by the time we called him by his first name. I'd be kind of disap-pointed if we never got the chance to be on a first-name basis."

The thundering sound in her ears, she realized, was her own heartbeat. There was something in his tone of voice that made the words seem so personal. Lifting her hand, she let it flutter around her throat. For several tense seconds it seemed as if the world had gone still, waiting for her to answer.

With an effort borne of practice, she recovered her composure. She would not allow this man to discomfort her to the point of foolishness. "You may very well be right, Major," she said evenly. "Nevertheless, I refuse to let the war or the people who caused it force me into abandoning my principles. One day this madness will be over, and those of us who survive will have to go on with our lives the way they were before. How we behave during this time of turmoil will dictate how successful we are in that endeavor."

"And you really believe that?"

Try as she might, she could not meet that penetrating gaze. "Believe what?"

"That everything will be the same as it was before once the war is over."

"If I didn't firmly believe that, I'm not sure I could cope with everything." Even as she said the words, she knew the futility of the sentiment. How could things ever be the same? The war was changing everybody in ways they had never imagined.

"Then, for your sake, I sure hope you're right." He cleared his throat, then added, "Corporal Barrows told me that he met Beryl Pierce at a dance hall in North Horsham. He admitted to messing around with her . . . his own words . . . but then she'd caused some kind of trouble with his girlfriend, and he dumped her."

"Did he say what kind of trouble?"

Major Monroe sighed. "Yes, ma'am. Apparently Beryl Pierce called the corporal's girlfriend and told her that she'd spent the night with him."

"Oh, dear." Elizabeth quickly shifted her gaze to the wall of windows in front of her.

"The girlfriend dumped him, of course, and so he dumped Beryl."

"He got no more than he deserved, really," Elizabeth murmured. "After all, what could he expect when he was playing around with two girls at once?"

"Yes, ma'am." The major cleared his throat again. "All this happened about two weeks ago. So he couldn't have been responsible for the young lady's condition. Corporal

Barrows swears he never saw Beryl Pierce after that day. End of story."

"Not quite." Elizabeth turned her head and met his gaze head on.

"Ma'am?"

"You're forgetting someone. What about Corporal Barrows's girlfriend? That young lady must have been extremely jealous and very angry with Beryl Pierce. Certainly as angry as Robert Barrows must have been when Beryl broke up his association with this woman. Someone who might possibly have been angry enough to hurt her, wouldn't you say?"

Major Monroe looked uncomfortable again. "It's possible, I guess."

"I don't suppose he told you her name?"

The major sighed. "No, ma'am. He didn't."

"I see." Elizabeth let the seconds tick by while she watched the conflicting expressions cross his face.

Finally he said abruptly, "I guess you want me to ask him for her name."

She let out her breath. "Would you? Thank you so much, Major. That would be a tremendous help."

Earl Monroe shook his head. "I don't know what brand of sweet talk you're using, Lady Elizabeth, but I want you to know if it were anyone else asking me to do this, I'd tell them to go to . . . heck."

"You can say hell, Major," Elizabeth said cheerfully. "I often do." She felt wonderful, as if someone had turned on the sunshine inside the room. It was a warm, effervescent feeling of well-being and was caused entirely by the major's last comment. The knowledge she was advancing on forbidden territory only made it all the more exciting.

CHAPTER

❦ 14 ❦

Elizabeth had been taking her meals with Violet and Martin in the spacious kitchen ever since her parents' funeral, when sitting alone in the dining room had so depressed her that she'd been unable to eat.

It was Violet's idea, and it was meant to last only for a short while until Elizabeth recovered from the shocking death of her family. Although Martin had vehemently revealed his displeasure at this scandalous departure from protocol, Elizabeth had eagerly accepted the suggestion.

Despite Violet's broad hints and Martin's frequent muttering about lack of propriety, however, she had stubbornly refused to return to that solitary chair at the end of the vast table that could and often had easily seated forty guests.

She was enjoying her light supper that evening when the bell in the kitchen jangled, indicating a visitor at the front door.

"I hope they haven't come back for more saucepans," Violet grumbled as she got up from her seat. "I don't know how I'm supposed to cook meals without saucepans."

"I do believe it's my duty to answer the door." Martin struggled to his feet. "Give me a moment to find my glasses, and I'll be right there."

"Your glasses are on your nose as usual." Violet hurried across the floor. "I have to go upstairs for a moment, anyway, so I might as well answer the door while I'm up there." She sent Elizabeth a meaningful look and rolled her eyes up at the ceiling before disappearing.

Martin carefully lowered himself onto the chair again. "It isn't Violet's place to answer the door, madam. Doors are opened and visitors greeted by the butler. What will people think?"

Elizabeth leaned forward and patted his hand. "Don't worry about it, Martin. People make allowances nowadays."

"I don't want people to make allowances. Your mother would be most upset if she could see you sitting here in the kitchen with me while the housekeeper answers the door. What is the world coming to? That's what I want to know."

"That's something we all want to know." Elizabeth gave him a fond smile. "I'm quite sure Mother would be happy to know you take such good care of me. She was always telling me how utterly reliable you are, and how I could count on you to offer your services whenever they are needed."

For a moment Martin's eyes looked almost shrewd. "That was before senility crept in. Although I hate to admit it, Lady Elizabeth, I am not the man I used to be. Far from it."

Elizabeth felt uncomfortable. She and Violet assumed that Martin was not aware of their efforts to make him continue to feel indispensable. Martin had always had a great deal of pride, and justifiably so. It was heartbreaking to think that he might realize just how dependent he had become on them.

Her concern faded when he added, "For instance, I can't ride that pesky bicycle anymore."

"Martin, to the best of my knowledge, you have never ridden a bicycle in your life."

His face brightened. "I haven't? Well, that would explain it, then, wouldn't it. I was wondering why I couldn't get those pedals to go round."

Elizabeth frowned. "What bicycle are you talking about? You don't mean the one belonging to Desmond, do you? That's the only bicycle I've seen around here."

"I'm talking about the red one, madam, that's always by the wall out there. The one with the little carriage fastened to it. I must admit, none of the bicycles I've ever seen before had carriages attached to them. Must be one of those newfangled inventions that are always popping up nowadays."

"Martin, that's my motorcycle. The pedals don't turn around. There's an engine that drives the wheels."

"An engine?"

"Yes, an engine. You have to turn it on." To her immense relief Violet returned before she had to explain the intricacies of a kick-start engine.

"It's Prince Charming again," Violet said, making no effort to conceal her disapproval. "I left him in the library. Making a blinking habit of calling in, isn't he? Don't they have telephones at that base?"

Elizabeth jumped to her feet. In her hurry, her hand caught the edge of her cup and sent it flying off the saucer. She retrieved it and set it down with utmost care. "I imagine there isn't much privacy at the base."

"Why on earth should he need privacy?"

Elizabeth sighed. "He's the person helping me to find out who killed Beryl Pierce."

"Someone killed Beryl Pierce?" Martin shot to his feet with surprising speed. "When did this happen?"

"A few days ago, Martin." Elizabeth looked at Violet, who was staring at her with a stormy expression on her face.

"Why are you messing about with this murder?" she demanded. "Why aren't the police doing their job?"

"Murder? Good lord, we're worse off than I thought. We must have new locks and bolts put on all the doors at once. I'll see to it. I knew those Germans would get here sooner or later." Martin shuffled as fast as his fading agility would allow and disappeared through the door.

Elizabeth stared after him. "You don't think he'll try to change the locks, do you?"

"By the time he's halfway up the stairs he'll have forgotten where he was going. What I want to know is why you didn't tell me you and this American major have been poking your noses into police business. That's a good way to get into trouble, I'd say."

Sometimes, Elizabeth thought with faint resentment, Violet could sound like both her parents rolled into one. "I didn't tell you because I knew you'd do exactly what you're doing," she said calmly. "I wanted to spare you the worry."

She could have said that it was none of Violet's business what she did, but if she did that, the housekeeper would go off in one of her huffs, and the tension would be unbearable for days. Besides, Violet meant well. And it was her own fault, Elizabeth reminded herself. Since she'd always treated Violet like a member of the family instead of an employee, she couldn't really be too surprised if she acted like one.

"Spare me the worry? What about the worry I'd feel if this murderer knew you were chasing him and decided to get rid of you as well? How do you think I'd feel then?"

Elizabeth crossed the room to the door. "Please, Violet, try not to worry. I'm not doing anything the least bit dangerous. Really. I'm just talking to a few people, that's all."

"I'm not so sure. How do you know this Major Monroe is safe to be alone with?"

"Because I trust him." She looked back at Violet. "We have to start trusting these people sometime. Especially if they're going to be our guests for a while."

"Uninvited guests, I might say."

Elizabeth smiled. "Cheer up, Violet. It's not going to be nearly as bad as you think it will be."

Violet sat down with a thump. "I just hope and pray you're right."

So did she, Elizabeth thought, as she hurried up the stairs. The closer the time came to the Americans moving in, the more nervous she got about it. But there wasn't a great deal she could do about it now.

When she opened the door of the library, she saw Major Monroe sitting on a straight-backed chair by the fireplace, a book open on his lap.

He leapt to his feet as she entered, with an expression she could only describe as guilt. "Hope you don't mind," he said, holding up the book, "but it caught my eye, and before I knew it I was hooked."

She smiled. "You haven't read it? *Wind in the Willows*

is required reading in our schools. It's one of my favorite books. You can borrow it if you like."

"Really?" He looked a little self-conscious. "You won't think I'm nuts for wanting to read a children's book?"

"Not at all. It's a classic and, from an adult's perspective, a very astute if somewhat ironic view of life. I think you'll enjoy it."

"I'll look forward to reading it." He waited for her to be seated before adding, "I hope you don't mind me coming back so soon. I didn't want to discuss this on the telephone."

"Of course not. Can I offer you some sherry? Or perhaps a martini? I think there's some gin left in the cellar."

"Nothing, thanks. I have to get back shortly."

"I assume you have some more news for me?"

"Yes." He sat down on the edge of the chair again. "I talked to Corporal Barrows again."

Elizabeth could tell that he was uncomfortable and did her best to put him at ease. "And he answered your questions?"

Earl Monroe stared down at the book in his hands. "Corporal Barrows was under the impression he could not be charged under British law. When I assured him that the British police would be allowed to question him, he was a little more cooperative."

"So what did he say? Was he aware that Beryl was expecting a child?"

"I have to ask for your promise not to repeat to the police anything I'm about to tell you. I gave my promise to Corporal Barrows that everything he told me would be confidential. If the police get a warrant to question him, then that's a different matter. I guess it will be up to him, then, what he tells them."

"I have one question for you first."

Major Monroe sighed heavily. "Okay, shoot."

"Do you think that Corporal Barrows killed Beryl Pierce?"

"No, ma'am. I do not. I'd stake my life on it."

The answer was swift and decisive, and after a moment's hesitation, she said quietly, "You have my promise, Major."

"Thank you, Lady Elizabeth. I appreciate that. According to Corporal Barrows, Beryl Pierce approached him with the news that she was pregnant with his child. Barrows swears the baby couldn't be his. His story is that he spent only one night with the girl, after an argument with his girlfriend. He couldn't ... er ... perform, because he was drunk. He left the next morning before she woke up."

Feeling every bit as embarrassed as the major looked, Elizabeth fixed her gaze on the chandelier in the middle of the room. "I see. Do you believe him?"

"Yes, ma'am. I do. Barrows told me that he lied the first time we talked. He did see Beryl Pierce again, the day before she died. He met her in town that Saturday afternoon, after she sent him a note saying if he didn't meet her, she was going to cause trouble for him at the base."

"I thought he was confined to the base that entire weekend."

"He was, ma'am. Which is why I believe he's telling the truth now. That little confession is going to cost him. Anyway, Beryl Pierce told Barrows he'd have to marry her, and he told her he couldn't marry anyone. He was already married. When he left her that afternoon, she was alive and well. After questioning a few of the men, I established that he slept in his quarters that night and didn't leave the base again until long after the body was found."

"And since Beryl was alive on Sunday morning, that would certainly give him an alibi."

"Yes, ma'am. That's how I see it."

She could hear the relief in his voice. She was relieved herself, even though she didn't entirely believe Robbie's story. There was a little matter of a letter he wrote to Beryl, indicating she'd meant a good deal more to him than he was ready to admit. His alibi seemed strong, however, and as much as she despised a man who could cheat on his unsuspecting wife that way, she would have hated to be instrumental in having one of Earl Monroe's men arrested.

"I'm sorry that you haven't found your murderer, Lady Elizabeth, but I have to tell you I'm real happy that it wasn't Corporal Barrows."

"Believe it or not, Major, so am I."

She lowered her gaze and found him watching her. "I believe you," he said quietly. "But I have to ask that you not involve me in any more of your investigation. This whole thing has been . . . tough."

She nodded, feeling dejected again for some reason. "Of course, Major."

"Can I make a suggestion?"

"Please do."

"Let the police handle this. Murder is serious business and no place for a woman like you."

She raised her chin. "I'm very good at taking care of myself, Major Monroe."

"I'm sure you are and I don't mean you're incapable or anything. You are one of the strongest ladies I've ever met, and that includes my wife. It's just that when some-one isn't qualified to do a dangerous job, that's when he can run into trouble. And I'd hate to see you get hurt. Ma'am."

Aware that she was staring at him, she quickly lowered her gaze. She hadn't understood anything he'd said past the words *my wife*. He was *married?* Of course he was married. A man who was as charming and good-looking as he was had to be married. She just hadn't thought about it, that was all. Not that it mattered, anyway. She was being ridiculous. Why should it make any difference to her if he had a wife?

"Ma'am?"

She pulled herself together. "I . . . I'm sorry, Major, I was thinking about poor Beryl and how devastating it must have been for her to discover she was pregnant." The lie slipped easily off her tongue, and Earl Monroe actually looked quite relieved.

"Okay. I just didn't want to offend you, that's all."

"Not at all." She stood up, trying to ignore the ache of disappointment that shouldn't be there. "Thank you so much, Major Monroe. I do appreciate you taking the time to talk to your corporal. I can imagine how difficult that must have been for you both."

"You're welcome, ma'am. I'm just glad we got everything cleared up." He moved toward the door, then paused, looking back at her. "I sure hope you'll think about what I said, about letting the police handle this."

She smiled through the shadow that seemed to have been cast over her. "I will. It doesn't seem as if I'm getting anywhere, anyway. Maybe it's time I let the police take over."

He smiled back, momentarily dazzling her. "I think that's a real good decision on your part, ma'am." He turned to go, and she held up her hand.

"By the way, Major, did you by any chance remember

to ask Corporal Barrows the name of his ex-girlfriend?"

The look he gave her was so reproachful she felt guilty. "Yes, ma'am, as a matter of fact I did. The girl is a recruitment officer for the Land Army. Her name is Carol Simmons."

Of course. She should have known. The dance hall in North Horsham. And what was it Carol had said with that caustic note in her voice? *She was throwing herself at everyone who looked at her, if you know what I mean.*

It would appear that Carol knew Beryl Pierce a little better than she'd been willing to admit. In which case, perhaps it would be worth another little visit to North Horsham.

She heard the front door close behind Major Monroe and sighed. All of a sudden, playing detective didn't seem quite so much fun anymore.

CHAPTER

❈ 15 ❈

Carol Simmons seemed ill at ease when Elizabeth once more entered the cluttered office. She stared at her visitor with a sort of closemouthed defiance that quickly evaporated when Elizabeth explained her position.

"You can either talk to me," she said, sitting herself down on the rickety chair in front of the desk, "or you can talk to the police. I assure you, I'm much more approachable."

"What do you want to know?" Carol began on a note of belligerence. "I've told you everything I know."

"I don't think you have." Elizabeth fastened her gaze on the young woman's face. "For instance, you neglected to tell me that you knew Beryl Pierce quite well. In fact, you lost your boyfriend to her. Corporal Robert Barrows, I believe, stationed at the American air base."

Carol's face went ashen. "Who told you that?"

"I don't think that's important right now." Elizabeth

softened her tone. "Why did you really give Beryl your telephone number? It certainly wasn't because she wanted to join the Land Army, was it."

Two spots of red appeared in Carol's pale cheeks. "I didn't give my number to her," she muttered. "I just told you that before to keep Robbie out of trouble. Beryl must have taken that from out of his jacket."

Elizabeth stared at her for a moment, then settled herself more comfortably on her chair. "I think perhaps it's time you told me the whole story."

Carol stared at the papers in front of her for the longest time, then said with a shrug, "All right. You know most of it, anyway. Beryl and I used to go to school together. She must have seen me at the dance with Robbie and took a fancy to him." A faint smile flicked across her face. "Not that I can blame her. He's really good-looking. Over six feet tall and shoulders like an ox. And the best dancer I've ever danced with. All the girls were watching us out there on the dance floor." She paused, her mind obviously returning to that night.

After a moment Elizabeth prompted, "And Beryl?"

"Beryl came up to our table and sat down, started talking like we were old friends. Robbie and I tried to ignore her. I'd just moved into this office, and they'd given me a new telephone number. I scribbled it down on a blank form I had in my handbag and gave it to Robbie. He put it in his uniform jacket, which was hanging over the back of his chair. Right after that Beryl got up with her drink in her hand and spilled some of it on his jacket."

"On purpose?"

Carol shrugged. "I didn't think so at the time, but she must have done. Robbie threw a fit, and Beryl was going on and on about how sorry she was, and trying to dry it with her handkerchief and everything. Anyway, Robbie wanted to leave after that, and I was choked because I'd got all dressed up for that dance and we'd only just got there. So we had a big row about it. Robbie got really angry and left, so I stayed at the dance without him."

Elizabeth thought she understood now. "So you think that Beryl took your telephone number out of Robbie's pocket while she was drying it? Why would she want to do that?"

"I suppose she wanted my telephone number so she could call me to tell me she and Robbie had spent the night together. I think she had it all planned right from the moment she sat at that table. When I talked to Robbie about it, he told me he went to the pub after the dance and drank himself silly. He remembers seeing Beryl in the pub but doesn't remember going home with her. He woke up early in the morning, let himself out of the house, and went back to the base. He swore he was too drunk to do anything with her, but I couldn't trust him after that, could I? So I had to break it all off."

Elizabeth filtered the information through her mind. It all made sense and coincided with what Robbie had told Earl Monroe. "When did all this happen?"

"Two weeks ago last Saturday. It seems like months now. I really miss Robbie."

Elizabeth wondered if Carol knew Robbie was married. It wasn't really her place to tell her that, but on the other hand, it might help the poor girl get over him more quickly. Deciding to leave that for the time being, she went back to the story Carol had told her. "You're saying that Beryl followed Robbie to the pub that night, then."

"Yes, I am. I think she got him drunk, then took him home with her, just to break us up."

"And you're convinced that the only time Robbie was with Beryl was that one night?"

Carol nodded vigorously. "Yes, m'm. Of course, when I found out Robbie was married, I realized I couldn't believe everything he'd said. But I really don't think he was that interested in Beryl. He didn't even like her that much. I could tell that at the dance. He only went back with her to the house because he was angry at me."

Elizabeth opened her handbag and took out the letter Robbie had written to Beryl. "I think you should take a look at this. It might change your mind."

Carol read the letter, and when she raised her head again, tears brimmed in her eyes. "Where'd you get this?"

"Beryl's bedroom." Elizabeth felt sorry for disillusioning the girl, but she had to be sure Carol was telling her the whole story.

"This isn't Beryl's letter." Carol folded it up again, but held onto it instead of handing it back to Elizabeth. "This letter was written to me. If Beryl had it, she must have stolen it from Robbie's pocket. It must have been there when she took the form with my telephone number."

"Are you certain about that?"

"I'm positive." Carol opened the letter again. "See this line Robbie wrote about the smell of lavender? That was a joke just between us. He never would have said that to anyone else." Carol suddenly buried her head in her hands. "I can't believe she's dead. She was a bitch, and I hated her for what she did, but I wouldn't want her dead." She lifted her face again. "Robbie didn't kill her, Lady Elizabeth. I'd stake my life on that. He's a bit hot-headed, like most of them Yanks, but he wouldn't kill no one. I'd swear to it."

Elizabeth pursed her lips. The woman certainly seemed genuine enough, but she'd given a very good performance the last time she'd questioned her. She was either looking at a maligned and very distressed woman, or a clever actress and a possible murderer. Which was it? "Did you, by any chance, run into Beryl after your breakup with Robbie?"

The red dots spread over Carol's cheeks. "You think I killed her?"

"I think you might have had a good reason to want her dead. After all, Beryl had spent the night with a man you were obviously fond of, and had caused your breakup."

"That's silly. I would never kill someone over a boyfriend. You think I'm stupid? No man is worth that."

Elizabeth heartily agreed. "Then perhaps you can tell me how you knew Robbie was married. Did he tell you that? According to his story, Beryl didn't know herself until the day before she was killed."

Carol's eyes widened in shock. "You talked to Robbie?"

"A friend of mine talked to him. He said he told Beryl last Saturday afternoon that he was married."

"She must have rang me right away," Carol murmured. "Miserable cow."

Elizabeth leaned forward. "Beryl rang you last Saturday afternoon?"

"Yes, right before I closed the office. She was crying and said that Robbie told her he was married, and she thought I should know, like she was doing me a favor." Carol shook her head. "I think she was just making sure I didn't go back to him."

"What time was that?"

"Round about six, I think."

"Did she say where she was or where she was going?"

"She didn't get the chance. I hung up on her, didn't I."

Frustrated, Elizabeth relaxed her tense shoulders. She had one more question for Carol Simmons, but she already had an idea of the answer. "Can you tell me where you were last Sunday morning?"

Carol's eyes suddenly blazed fire. "Are you accusing me? I didn't have anything to do with her murder. I swear it. Anyway, if you'll pardon me for saying so, m'm, this really isn't any of your business, is it. Shouldn't the police be asking these questions?"

Elizabeth nodded. "You're quite right. Would you rather talk to the police, then?"

Carol backed down in a hurry. "No, I wouldn't." She drummed her fingers on the desk. "All right. If you must know, I was in bed Sunday morning. Or most of it, anyway. I was dancing until late Saturday night, got home late, and slept late. You can ask me mum. She brought me a cup of tea in bed that morning. I had breakfast after that, then I went out in the fields to help out some of the girls. I was there all afternoon."

There it was. As she'd pretty much expected. It would be simple enough to confirm Carol's story. The end of another promising lead. Elizabeth got up slowly from her chair. "Thank you, Miss Simmons, for being so candid with me. I appreciate you taking the time to talk to me."

Carol rose, too, wariness on her face. "Are you going to tell the police?"

"If you're asking if I'm going to tell them about you and Robbie, the answer is probably not. Since it appears that they would be wasting their time by pursuing that particular line of investigation, I see no point in bringing it up. You might as well keep the letter, too."

When Carol Simmons smiled, she looked extraordinarily beautiful. In spite of her size, she was an attractive woman. Elizabeth found herself hoping that the young lady would soon find herself someone more worthy upon whom she could bestow her affection.

Marlene stood at the corner sink in the rear of the narrow hairdresser's and stared at her sister's image in the mirror. Well pleased with her efforts, she laid down her comb and folded her arms. "There. I think it makes you look a lot older."

Polly leaned forward in her chair and frowned at her reflection. She studied the new hairdo for a moment or two in silence. Her long, straight hair was now pulled back from her face and fastened into a French twist at the back of her head.

"Here, look at the back of it." Marlene twisted her around in the chair and held up a hand mirror. "So what do you think?"

"Makes me face look thinner."

"Makes your eyes look bigger."

"Makes me nose look bigger an' all."

"Makes you look older, though."

Polly swung around again to face the mirror. "I don't know if I can get it up by myself."

"You'll have to learn how. Of course, if you let me cut it for you, it would be easier to manage."

"No!" Polly put both hands on her head. "I'm not having it cut off."

"Then this will have to do."

"It does make me look older." Polly lifted her chin. "Just wait until Sam sees this. He'll never guess I'm only fifteen."

Marlene felt a stab of uneasiness. "I wish you'd just tell Sam the truth. No good ever comes of telling lies."

"Now you sound like Ma." Polly stretched her neck

and swept her face from side to side. "It does look rather gorgeous, if I say so myself."

"Thanks," Marlene said dryly. "How long are you going to keep it up?"

"Until I go to bed. I'll have to put it up again in the morning, though."

"No, I mean letting Sam think you're twenty. He's going to find out eventually, you know."

"Not if you don't tell him. Besides, by the time he finds out, he'll be so potty over me it won't make any difference."

Marlene rolled her eyes up at the ceiling. "What about telling him you were secretary to Lady Liza? He's going to know you were lying about that when he moves in there and sees you cleaning out the toilet."

Polly scowled back at her in the mirror. "He's not going to see me, is he."

"Then why are you worrying about your hair?"

"Because I've got a plan."

"What kind of plan?"

Polly shrugged. "I'm going to ask Lady Liza if I can work part-time in her study. She's always complaining that she can't find anything. I can do some filing and maybe write some letters and help pay the bills."

Marlene laughed. "You don't know how to do all that."

"I can learn, can't I? That's what people do, isn't it? They're not born knowing how to do those things. They have to learn somewhere."

"All right, all right, don't get your knickers in a twist." Marlene sat down in the chair next to Polly. "You're going to a lot of trouble for this bloke. I hope he's worth it."

Polly grinned. "So do I."

"What if he's married? They say half of them are married and lie about it."

"So what if he is? I'm not thinking about marrying him and going off to America or anything. I just want a bit of fun, that's all. And I like Sam. He makes me laugh."

"Well, you'd better hope Ma doesn't find out about him or you'll be laughing on the wrong side of your face."

Polly sighed. "I can't wait to be eighteen like you. You could go to Scotland and get married any time you wanted."

"Yeah, but I wouldn't." Marlene stared anxiously at her sister. "Do be careful, Polly. I don't want to see you get into trouble."

Polly looked back at her image in the mirror. "Don't worry, I'll be careful. I'm just going to let Sam think I'm twenty for a little while, until he gets to know me better."

"Then you'll tell him the truth soon?"

"Just as soon as I think he can't live without me." Polly's laugh filled the whole shop. "Who says that wartime can't be fun?"

Elizabeth left the recruitment office feeling more than a little frustrated. Every clue she had followed so far seemed to lead to a dead end. Maybe she had been a little too quick in condemning George and Sid for their lack of progress in such matters. Investigating a crime, particularly a murder it would seem, was a lot more difficult than she'd envisioned.

There was, however, one more possible suspect in this tangle of events: the soldier who might have sent Beryl a one-way ticket to London. There was also another point that Elizabeth was anxious to clear up. According to Carol's story, if both she and Robbie were telling the truth, Beryl took Robbie home with her for the night. Elizabeth couldn't help wondering how he managed to get into and out of the house without Winnie hearing anything.

Seated in Winnie's cozy parlor a while later, Elizabeth recounted the entire story of Beryl's fling with Robbie Barrows. She made Winnie promise not to repeat anything to anyone, stilling her feelings of guilt with the reminder that her promise to the major was to withhold the information only from the police.

Winnie listened with mounting horror, especially when she heard that Beryl had actually brought in an American who had spent the night in her daughter's bedroom.

"You didn't hear them at all?" Elizabeth asked as Winnie sat with a dazed look on her face.

"Not a blooming thing." Winnie shook her head, as if trying to clear her thoughts. "I've been sleeping really heavy ever since I started taking the tablets."

Elizabeth sat up straighter. "Tablets?"

Winnie looked sheepish. "When Stan went away, I couldn't sleep at all, and the doctor gave me tablets to take, to help me sleep. They're very good. I'm never awake longer than half an hour after I take them, and I sleep like the dead until the next morning. I used to wait until Beryl got home before I took them, but lately she'd been getting home so late, and if I took them late I had trouble waking up the next day. That's probably why I didn't hear her and that bloody Yank come in the house."

"But you heard her the night before she died."

"Yes, I did. She came home early that night. That's why. I'd taken the tablets, but they hadn't had time to work." Winnie sighed. "So you don't think this Yank was the father of her baby?"

"I don't see how he could be." Elizabeth sipped her tea then set the cup down. "Both he and Carol said that he'd first met Beryl just two weeks before she died. The medical examiner said she was at least two months pregnant. My guess is that she knew she was pregnant the night she went to the dance hall in North Horsham. I think she was looking for an American to put the blame on, probably hoping he'd take her back to America with him. From what I hear, most of the girls in the village are hoping the same thing."

"Maybe, but most of them don't do what our Beryl did to get there. What her father will say when he hears all this I don't know." Winnie passed a hand across her forehead. "He should be here any day now. How am I going to tell him all this?"

"I'm sorry, Winnie." Elizabeth got to her feet. "I'm sorry I couldn't find Beryl's murderer."

Winnie looked startled. "You're not giving up, are you?"

"I really don't know what else I can do."

"Well, what about this Steve—the soldier in London who sent her the ticket? What about him?"

If there was one thing Elizabeth hated, it was to be thwarted by circumstances beyond her control. When she set out to do something, she wanted to see it through to the bitter end, no matter what it took to get there. To get this far in this miserable search for the poor child's murderer and come up against a dead end frustrated her immensely. "It would be like looking for a needle in a haystack," she said, gathering up her handbag and gloves. "All we have is a badge and a first name."

"Doesn't Amy know what he looks like?"

"I don't think she ever saw him. She was just going on what Beryl had told her."

"There has to be something you can do. George would never have found out everything you have so far. He hasn't even started looking. I think he's waiting for the inspector to get here, whenever that will be."

"Well, I've done the best I could. Unfortunately it wasn't enough. I suppose I'm not really cut out to be a detective."

"It's not like you to give up, m'm."

Elizabeth stood very still. "No," she said finally, "it's not, is it. Maybe there is something I can do. We'll have to see."

She moved to the door, knowing that it was a futile hope she was giving Winnie. "Maybe there's someone in Whitehall who can help me. But I wouldn't get your hopes too high if I were you. The chances are we might never find this Steve, and if he is the murderer, we might never know for sure what really happened that Sunday morning."

"If he is the murderer," Winnie said fiercely, "you'll find him. I just know you will, Lady Elizabeth. You have your father's grit and determination. You'll bring my daughter's killer to justice, I know you will."

Elizabeth walked slowly down the long garden path. She thought she knew now how Major Monroe must feel when leading his men into a dangerous mission. All those men depending on him. It was a frightening prospect.

Winnie might not be depending on her for her life, but Elizabeth was quite certain that if Beryl's murderer was not found and brought to justice, Winnie would be tormented by the injustice of that for the rest of her life. She could not let that happen. Somehow she had to find a British soldier named Steve serving in the Royal Engineers and stationed in London.

She passed the postman on the way up to the manor. Cyril Appleby was a pleasant man who knew everyone's business in the village, mostly because he read the postcards that arrived at the post office. He'd also been seen holding sealed envelopes up to the light. No one had ever actually accused him of opening the mail, but his knowledge of people's family business was a little too intimate to have been picked up by idle gossip.

Cyril waved to her as Elizabeth roared by, a feat that almost cost him his balance on the ancient bicycle that had been his faithful steed for as long as Elizabeth could remember. The spokes were rusty and bent, the saddle was almost worn through, and the crooked handlebars caused Cyril to weave all over the road instead of hugging the hedgerows, putting him in dire danger of being mowed down by a passing army jeep. Nevertheless, Cyril clung to his ancient machine, saying he could never get used to riding a new bicycle.

Elizabeth answered his wave and continued on her way, struggling with the enormity of the task ahead of her. She had friends in Whitehall, thanks to her volunteer work in the city, but she wasn't at all sure any of them had the means at their disposal to track down one soldier in an entire regiment.

Violet opened the door to her, and she stepped inside the cool walls of the Manor House, forgetting her troubles for the moment in the sheer pleasure of being home again.

"You just missed George Dalrymple," Violet said as Elizabeth pulled off her gloves. "He wanted to know where you were. I told him you were in North Horsham shopping for when the Yanks come. He got real excited when I told him about our uninvited guests. Wanted me to ask them if they could get him some American comics. I asked him what was wrong with our English ones. You know what he said?"

Only half listening, Elizabeth murmured, "No, tell me."

"He said that English comics were for children. American ones, he says, have big busty women in them, and they're meant for grown-up men. Can you believe that? I told him that was disgusting. I hope they don't bring those things in here, I told him, or they're going right in the fireplace where they belong."

"What did he say to that?"

"Got all hoity-toity, didn't he. Said it was against the law to destroy someone else's property. I told him it was against the law to bring filthy comics into my house. That shut him up."

For some reason it was on the tip of Elizabeth's tongue to point out that the Manor House was actually hers and that Violet was there by virtue of being employed there, but thankfully sanity returned and, ashamed of her pettiness, she banished the thought. "I'm sure he didn't mean to offend you," she said instead.

Violet gave her a sharp look. "You look tired, Lizzie. Come downstairs, and I'll make you a nice cup of tea."

She wasn't tired, Elizabeth thought as she followed the housekeeper down to the kitchen. She felt beaten. This whole investigation had started out with such promise. She'd actually quite enjoyed chasing down the clues and talking to the suspects. She'd particularly enjoyed her little chats with Major Monroe. But now it seemed as if her efforts had all been for nothing, and even Earl Monroe wanted nothing more to do with the case. Or her, more than likely, now that she'd made such a pest of herself.

She slumped down at the kitchen table. "You know, Violet, I think I'll have a glass of sherry instead of tea. It might help to brighten me up a bit."

"If you ask me, you're taking on too much," Violet grumbled. "Running around here and there trying to find out who done in Beryl Pierce when you should be here at home worrying about how we're going to get the chimneys cleaned before winter sets in."

Elizabeth gathered her thoughts with a start. "Did you get the curtains from the east wing washed?"

If Violet realized she'd deliberately changed the subject, she gave no sign of it. "Yes, I did. Polly helped me wash them. What a job that was, too, I might tell you. Got them all hung up on the line out there. I just hope the wind doesn't blow too hard, or it will rip those curtains to bits. It was all we could do not to rip them when we pegged them on the line. I just—" She broke off as the telephone rang, shattering the peace of the kitchen. "Now who's that?"

She hurried over to the wall and lifted off the receiver.

Watching her, Elizabeth tried not to hope that it was Major Monroe, ringing with some piece of news that would shed some light on the mystery. Or just simply ringing.

"She's resting right now. . . . All right, just a minute. I'll get her." Violet held out the receiver to Elizabeth. "It's Winnie. She says it's important."

Elizabeth took the telephone and pressed it to her ear. "Winnie? This is Lady Elizabeth. What is it?"

"I'm down at the Tudor Arms, Lady Elizabeth. I thought I'd better call you right away."

Winnie's voice sounded urgent, and Elizabeth's spine tingled. "Something's happened?"

"There's another letter for Beryl. It's from London. From that Steve. I think you'd better take a look at it."

CHAPTER 16

Elizabeth curled her fingers tighter around the telephone. "Did you open the letter yet, Winnie? What does it say?"

"I opened it, m'm. But I don't really think I should talk about it here in the pub. I'm really sorry to bother you like this, but I think you might want to see this letter. Could you possibly come back down to the house, or would you rather I bring it up there? I'd have to wait for the bus—"

"No, that's quite all right, Winnie. I have some errands to run, so I'll stop by on my way out." She replaced the receiver and turned to see Violet's face wreathed in disapproval.

"You're not going out again? You just got home. Dinner's almost ready. I got shepherd's pie in the oven."

Elizabeth glanced at the clock. "Keep it warm, Violet, there's a dear. I won't be long, I promise."

"I think you're spending entirely too much time down

at that Winnie's cottage." Violet turned down the heat in the oven. "No wonder you're getting behind with the bookkeeping. I don't know what people will think, really I don't. It's not proper for a lady of your standing to be running around the village like this, in and out of people's cottages. Rita Crumm said you were out on the coast road with them. Said you were taking training so you could help kill the Germans when they came ashore for the invasion." Violet crossed her arms and fixed her stern gaze on Elizabeth's face. "I didn't believe her, of course. I hope you're going to tell me that's not true."

"Of course it's not true." Elizabeth pulled her light cotton jacket from the back of her chair and slipped it on over her frock. "Well, I suppose I was out there—"

Violet's gasp of outrage stopped Elizabeth for a moment, then she doggedly continued. "But I most certainly did not participate in any training. I happened to run into them, that's all."

"Not literally, I hope."

"No, but it was a miracle I didn't." Elizabeth crossed the room to the door. "One of these days Rita Crumm is going to cause a real disaster with her misguided efforts to be a hero."

Violet grinned. "And you can't wait for that day, can you."

Elizabeth shrugged. "I wouldn't want to see anyone get hurt." She met Violet's gaze and laughed. "All right, I admit I'd like to see Rita Crumm fall flat on her face. Figuratively speaking, of course."

Violet nodded. "Of course."

Elizabeth decided it was time to leave before she incriminated herself. It took her only a minute or two to retrieve her handbag and gloves from her room. As she headed back to the stairs, however, Polly appeared from the bathroom, bucket in one hand, mop in the other.

For a moment Elizabeth didn't recognize her. Her hair had been twisted up into a sophisticated style that looked much too mature for a young girl. It was really too bad these girls couldn't wait to grow up. If only they could realize that being an adult was not nearly as exciting and mysterious as they imagined.

Polly looked almost scared as she plopped the bucket down and advanced toward her. "Can I have a word with you, Lady Elizabeth?"

Elizabeth felt a pang of apprehension. Surely Polly wasn't going to give in her notice? If so, she couldn't deal with it right now. Hoping to put off what would amount to disaster, she shook her head. "I'm in rather a hurry, Polly. Can it wait until this afternoon?"

"Oh, I won't keep you a minute, m'm. I was just wondering if I could help you out in the study now and then."

Elizabeth paused and frowned at her. "I don't understand, Polly. I thought you already cleaned the study. Isn't that one of your normal duties?"

"Oh, yes, m'm. It is. I mean, I do." Polly wound the long wet strands of the mop around her fingers. "What I was wondering, m'm, was if I could perhaps help you write letters, pay the bills, that sort of thing."

All she could think about was the fact that Polly wasn't leaving after all. She smiled her relief. "Well, thank you, Polly, but I really don't need any help. Besides, you're always complaining that you have too much to do now." She snapped her fingers. "By the way, as long as we're addressing the subject, I was wondering if perhaps you could come in full time when the Americans move in. In spite of Major Monroe's good intentions, I'm quite sure there'll be quite a lot more work to take care of with our house guests in the east wing."

"Yes, of course, m'm." Polly looked almost desperate in her eagerness. "In which case I'll have plenty of time to help you out in the study. Really. I won't disturb you or nothing, I promise. I just want to help, that's all."

The girl looked so distraught that Elizabeth felt quite sorry for her. She couldn't help feeling there was something behind Polly's request that the girl wasn't telling her, but she didn't have time to worry about it now. "I really don't know what you could do to help," she said, edging past her, "but I'll think about it, all right?"

Polly nodded, though she didn't look too reassured. "Thank you, Lady Elizabeth. I'm much obliged."

"Not at all." Elizabeth fled before she agreed to something she'd regret later.

Running down the stairs, she almost collided with Martin, who hovered in the shadows at the bottom, apparently trying to decide where he wanted to go next.

"Madam!" he exclaimed as she rushed past him, "is everything all right? You look as if someone is chasing you." He peered up the stairs in alarm. "The Germans haven't arrived, have they? I haven't got my sword with me to protect you."

"There are no Germans, Martin," Elizabeth called out breathlessly, "so you can stop worrying about your sword. Go on down to the kitchen. Violet has dinner almost ready." She flew out of the front door and down the steps, grimly reflecting that should the Germans arrive at the Manor House, Martin was going to need a great deal more than a sword for protection.

Hot on the heels of that thought came the reminder that with several American airmen in the house, she, Violet, and Martin would at least have some defense against the invaders. The notion made her feel almost lighthearted as she wheeled her way down the lane to Winnie's cottage.

When she arrived there, Winnie was hanging over the garden gate, obviously watching for her. "Oh, thank you for coming, m'm," she cried, the second Elizabeth climbed off her motorcycle. "Come on in. I've got the kettle on."

"Oh, no more tea, thank you, Winnie. I'll float away if I drink any more right now. Do tell me, though. What's in the letter?"

"Come inside, and I'll give it to you." Winnie scuttled up the path, then waited for Elizabeth to go in ahead of her.

The letter lay on the small table by the front door, where Winnie had apparently dropped it after reading it. She hadn't even stopped to put it back inside the envelope. "Here, m'm," she said, picking it up. "Read for yourself."

Elizabeth quickly scanned the lines scribbled unevenly across the blue-lined paper. In the very first sentence, Steve demanded to know why Beryl hadn't arrived in London. Apparently he'd waited over an hour at Liverpool Street Station for her. From what Elizabeth could understand from the untidy scrawl, the two of them had an appointment with someone to end Beryl's pregnancy. According to Steve, the so-called doctor she was supposed to meet was livid when Steve had told him Beryl hadn't turned up.

Elizabeth shuddered. "She was going to get rid of the baby? That poor child."

Winnie just nodded, her lips pressed tightly together.

In the next part of the letter, Steve told Beryl that he'd been thinking things over, and now regretted telling her he couldn't marry her.

*If you've changed your mind about getting rid of
the baby, I'm ready to get married. What I did was
wrong, I know that now, and it's up to me to put
things right. I really do love you, Beryl, and I'll be
a good father to our baby. Please let me know what
you think. All my love, Steve.*

Her heart aching, Elizabeth put down the letter and
picked up the envelope. Turning it over, she looked at
the date. It had been posted on the day after Beryl had
died. "He'll have to be informed, of course," she said,
dropping the envelope back on the table.

"I'll write and tell him." Winnie uttered a shuddering
sigh. "He was ready to marry our Beryl. She didn't have
to go through all that mess with that Yank. If only that
Steve had sent this letter sooner, our Beryl might still be
alive."

"I'm so sorry, Winnie. I know how you must feel."
Elizabeth patted the forlorn woman on the shoulder. "But
the fact remains that someone did kill Beryl. Only now
it appears we have run out of suspects."

Winnie took out her handkerchief and rubbed her nose.
"If only I hadn't taken those blinking tablets that Saturday night. I might have woken up earlier on Sunday
morning before Beryl left the house. I might have
stopped her wherever she was going, and she might never
have died."

"You've got to stop blaming yourself," Elizabeth said
sharply. "Beryl was killed for a reason, one we might
never know now. But whatever it was, it had nothing to
do with what you did or didn't do, and there is absolutely
no point in tormenting yourself. You have to accept what
happened and try to go on as best you can."

"I know you're right, m'm." Winnie sniffed loudly.

"But it would be so much easier if I knew who killed her and why he did it. It's like there's no real ending to this, isn't it."

"I'm sorry." Elizabeth wished she could think of something better to say than those two trite words. "Maybe the inspector will be able to find out who the culprit is when he gets here."

"If he gets here. He's probably much too busy to worry about what goes on in our little village." Winnie blew her nose and stuffed the handkerchief back in her apron pocket. "Well, I mustn't keep you, Lady Elizabeth. You've already spent far too much time on my troubles lately." She opened the door again to let her visitor out. "I really appreciate everything you've done. I'm just sorry I wasted your time."

"It's never a waste of time to help people in need." Elizabeth stepped out onto the path. "I just wish I could have found the answer to all this." She turned to go, then paused as she caught sight of a stocky figure tramping up the lane, dressed in the dark blue uniform of the Royal Navy. "Isn't that—" she began, but with a cry Winnie interrupted her.

"Stan! It's my Stan!"

Elizabeth watched as the stout woman tore down the path and through the gate. At the sight of her, the sailor dropped his duffel bag and held out his arms. Winnie rushed right into them, and he closed them around her. He held her close, while her sobs drifted on the wind to where Elizabeth stood, her own tears forming in her eyes at the sight.

She walked slowly down the path to the gate, then out to her motorcycle. The engine cut through the still air, startling the couple who still clung to each other in the middle of the road.

Elizabeth drew level with them and smiled at Winnie's husband. "Please accept my deepest sympathy for the loss of your daughter," she said, "and welcome home. Your wife needs you."

Apparently overcome, Stan Pierce nodded and drew his wife's trembling shoulders closer to his body.

Elizabeth left them there, sharing their grief together beneath the warm summer sky.

She took her time riding home. She needed the clean, fresh air rushing past her face with its tangy scent of the ocean to clear her mind. It was obvious Steve hadn't killed Beryl, since he'd mailed the letter from London the day after she'd died. Carol, Robbie, and Evan all had airtight alibis for the morning Beryl died.

So why did she still feel she was missing something important? Her conversation with Winnie kept playing through her mind. Something about the woman taking sleeping tablets bothered her. Elizabeth cast her mind back, to the day Winnie had first told her that Beryl was missing. What were Winnie's exact words?

"I didn't see her come in, but I heard her all right. I was half asleep, but I called out to her. She never answered me."

The thought hit her like a thunderclap. What if Beryl hadn't answered *because it wasn't Beryl who Winnie had heard?* Elizabeth's start of excitement almost unseated her. She grasped the handlebars more tightly and choked on the throttle. She had to think this through. She had to remember what else it was that Winnie had said.

"She was gone by the time I got up. Never made her bed before she went out neither. Whatever got her out of the house that early on a Sunday must have been really important."

Right after dinner, Elizabeth decided with mounting

excitement, she'd call the medical examiner. Stella Sheridan, the doctor's wife, had worked on several charity committees with her. It shouldn't be too difficult to ask the doctor one simple question.

Violet was happy to hear that Stan Pierce had arrived home at last. "Now perhaps you'll stop running down to Winnie's house every five minutes," she muttered as she drew the steaming pie from the oven. "Perhaps we can have our meals on time now. Martin has been drooling at that table for almost an hour."

"I beg your pardon?" Martin sniffed with contempt. "I do not drool. Saint Bernards drool. Butlers do not."

Violet dumped the dish on the table. "Well, just try to stop your mouth watering around that, if you can."

Martin picked up his serviette and dabbed at his mouth. "It's my false teeth," he muttered. "They always start dribbling whenever I smell food cooking."

Violet rolled her eyes. "Always got some excuse, you have." She piled the steaming, seasoned minced beef onto a dinner plate, then added an extra dollop of the fluffy mashed potatoes. After putting down the plate in front of Elizabeth, she filled another plate and set it in front of Martin.

"There, get this down your gullet and stop your complaining. You're bloody lucky to be getting meat at all, what with all the rationing and all. Though it seems a crime to me to put food like this on a Royal Doulton." She held up a clean plate and inspected it. "We should be eating venison or Dover sole on plates like this. What Lady Wellsborough would say if she could see us now, I dread to think."

Martin lifted his head. "Lady Wellsborough is back? Oh, my. Who opened the door to her? It wasn't I. Why wasn't it I? What will she think?" He struggled to get out of his chair. "I have to go to her at once. She will think I'm shirking in my duty."

"Sit down, you old fool," Violet said crossly. "Lady Wellsborough can't be here, can she, unless it's her ghost."

Martin's eyes widened, but he obediently sank back in his chair. "Ghosts? We are being haunted? I always suspected the Manor House was haunted, but I've never seen any of the ghosts. Where did you see them? I'll be willing to wager you saw them in the great hall. It's the perfect place for ghosts to wander."

"I bloody hope not," Violet muttered, sitting herself down in front of her own plate. "If we've got ghosts in the great hall, we'll have a few bloody Yanks running around in their underwear."

Martin's knife and fork descended on his plate with a clatter. "I say, Violet, that's a bit much. In front of madam, too. You really should watch your tongue."

Violet snorted, then glanced at Elizabeth. "You're awfully quiet. Something bothering you?"

Elizabeth shook her head. "Just preoccupied." With her knife she edged some more of the meat onto the back of her fork. "This is delicious, Violet."

Violet took a mouthful, then nodded in agreement. "Not bad. Could have used a little more salt."

"A lot more salt," Martin grumbled. "This tastes more like paper."

"Good, then I'll serve you the middle pages of the *Daily Mirror* tomorrow, since you can't tell the difference."

"I used to have fish and chips wrapped up in a newspaper when I was a child." Martin closed his eyes. "I can still remember the smell. It's been so long since I had fish and chips."

"Must be at least a bloody hundred years," Violet said nastily. "I'm surprised they had newspapers back then."

Elizabeth ignored their bickering. She was so used to listening to it at mealtimes it would be oddly quiet if they ever stopped. Instead she tried very hard to grasp at something that kept niggling in her mind, just beyond her reach. Something that someone had told her about Beryl, something that seemed important yet so elusive that it couldn't be significant. Or could it?

Anxious now to talk to the doctor, she cleaned the last of her plate and pushed her chair back.

"Where are you going now?" Violet demanded. "Not off again, are you? I was hoping you'd go over the east wing with me this afternoon, and tell me what you need done before the Americans move in."

"Americans? Why does everyone keep talking about Americans?" Martin laid his knife and fork down again. "Where are they, that's what I want to know. I haven't seen any Americans about. I'm sure I'd recognize one if I had."

Violet sighed. "They're not here yet, are they. You'll soon know when they get here, I can promise you that."

"Why? Are they bringing their horses? I don't think Desmond will like that at all."

"Desmond doesn't like anything that vaguely resembles work." Violet shook her head at him. "You don't have to worry, Martin, the cowboys have left their horses behind in America."

"Don't confuse him any more than necessary." Elizabeth rose from the table. "It's all right, Martin. The Americans will be moving in very soon now, but you really don't have to worry about it. They will be taking care of themselves."

"With Polly's help, no doubt," Violet muttered.

"I do hope they don't run into the ghosts," Martin said, looking worried.

Elizabeth abandoned the attempt to reassure him. "I need to ring someone," she said to Violet, "and then we'll take a look at the east wing."

"All right. I have the washing up to do, anyway. Thank goodness Polly's back. I'm going to need her."

"I've decided to have her come in every day once our guests are here," Elizabeth said, heading for the door. "I've already talked to her about it, and she's agreed."

Violet groaned. "Oh, Lord, I've got to put up with that twit every day? I'll never get anything done, that's for sure."

"Well, actually, she asked me if she could help out in the study."

"Polly? What can she do in there?"

Elizabeth shrugged. "Well, she could help out with the filing, I suppose. Heaven knows I could use some help."

"I hope you know what you're doing. If you ask me, it would be a big mistake having that girl mucking about with your papers. They'll end up in a worse mess than what you got now."

"Well, it won't hurt to try it for a while, I suppose." Deciding this was a good time to leave, Elizabeth let the door swing to behind her and hurried up the stairs. It was after two, so the doctor should have finished his rounds. She closed the door of the study, then thumbed through the directory. It took her only a minute or two to locate his number. Taking a deep breath, she hooked her finger and dialed.

The voice that answered her informed her she was the Sheridans' housekeeper.

"This is Lady Elizabeth Hartleigh Compton, from the

Manor House in Sitting Marsh. I'd like a word with Dr. Sheridan if he's there?"

"I'll see if he's in," the voice politely answered.

A few more minutes passed, then a gruff voice barked, "Lady Elizabeth? This is Dr. Sheridan. What can I do for you?"

Elizabeth hesitated, then said carefully, "Dr. Sheridan, I realize this is a lot to ask, but I have a question about the recent murder of Beryl Pierce. I was wondering if you could help me with it."

She waited through the long pause that followed, and crossed her fingers. Finally the doctor answered her.

"You know, of course that this is official police business. I'm not sure how much I can tell you."

"Well, perhaps you can tell me this. Is it at all possible that Beryl could have died before Sunday morning? Such as Saturday evening, for instance?"

Again a pause, then Dr. Sheridan said cautiously, "Entirely possible. As a matter of fact, if it hadn't been for Mrs. Pierce's statement that her daughter didn't leave the house until Sunday morning, I would have been convinced she'd been in the water all night."

Elizabeth could feel her heart thumping against her ribs. "Thank you, Dr. Sheridan. I appreciate your cooperation."

The doctor sounded worried when he answered. "Lady Elizabeth, I'm not sure what this is all about, but I must caution you that if you have information that could be helpful in this case, you must inform the police immediately."

"If you mean proof of guilt, Doctor, I'm afraid I can't help you. Just pure speculation, that's all."

"Nevertheless, knowing the constables as well as I do,

they might well be interested in your thoughts on the subject."

Elizabeth smiled. "I promise you, Dr. Sheridan, just as soon as I sort it all out in my mind, George Dalrymple will be the first to know."

She replaced the receiver and leaned back. The Queen Anne armchair, with its deep seat and winged sides, had been her father's favorite place on which to rest. As a child she had sat on his lap while he'd told her stories about dragons and princesses and brave knights saving the day.

More than once he'd told her that he could think more clearly when he sat in that chair. After he'd died, she'd spent hours just sitting there, recalling everything she could about the father she had idolized. Now it was her turn to concentrate, and she couldn't imagine a better place to be.

According to Winnie, she'd assumed that Beryl had spent the night in the house because she'd heard her close the front door. Also her bed had been slept in. But what if Beryl had died Saturday night, and it had been someone else entering the house that night? That could explain why Winnie received no answer when she called out.

The intruder could have gone up to Beryl's room, messed up the bed to make it look as if it had been slept in, then left to establish an alibi. Once Winnie's tablets had started working, she wouldn't have heard that person leave.

If she was right, Elizabeth thought, then it was a daring plan. The murderer was taking a big chance on getting in and out of the house without being seen. Unless he already knew about Winnie's tablets.

For a long time, Elizabeth sat there among the shadows

of ghosts who had sat in that room before her. Slowly the pieces fell into place, one by one. When she finally rose from the chair, it was all clear in her mind. All that was left to do now was set things in motion.

CHAPTER

✷ 17 ✷

Before she could do anything, Elizabeth reminded herself, she needed to run over to the east wing with Violet. Now that she had the entire picture clear in her mind, she could afford to wait an hour or two.

The east wing, however, could not wait. There were only two days left before the Americans moved in, and there was still so much to be done.

Standing in the doorway of the master suite, she took a critical look around the room. "The curtains look so much better," she told Violet. "But now the bedspread looks a little drab. I really think we should wash it."

"All right." Violet glanced out of the window. "I just hope the rain holds off long enough to dry it on the line."

"You will have Polly polish the furniture in here, won't you?" Elizabeth crossed the room and pulled open the doors of the heavy wardrobe. "I think we should hang some fresh mothballs in here. I should hate Major Monroe to find holes in his uniform."

She closed the doors again. "What about that lamp? Don't you think the shade is a little too flowery for a man? Perhaps we should exchange it for the one in the library. And that cushion will have to go. Much too fussy."

"Lizzie, will you please stop stewing about all this? It's only a few fly boys coming to stay, not the blinking king of England."

"They're visitors to our country. I just want to give them a good impression. I want them to feel at home here."

"And how many of them do you think live in a miniature version of Buckingham blinking Palace? Besides, I thought they were bringing in their own furniture."

"They are." Feeling defensive, Elizabeth reluctantly moved to the door. "I suppose you're right. There's no sense in getting too upset about a handful of American airmen."

"Good. I'm glad we got that settled." Violet followed her out into the hallway.

"But you were right about the air in the pipes. They do make such a beastly noise."

"Well, if it bothers them, maybe one or two of them will volunteer to do a little plumbing. We can live in hopes, anyway."

"Very well, I'll leave you and Polly to handle things, then." Elizabeth glanced at her watch. "Now I have to go out again. I don't know how long I'll be, but I should be home in time for supper."

Violet shook her head. "Gawd knows why they call you lady of the manor. You're never here."

"Well, after today I should be spending a little more

time at home." Elizabeth hurried down the stairs with Violet close behind her.

"Does that mean you're giving up playing detective?"

"It means," Elizabeth said as she reached the front door, "that I fully expect Beryl's murderer to be in the hands of the police by tomorrow."

"Go on!" Violet stared at her. "You know who did it? Who was it, then?" Her eager expression changed to alarm. "Here, you're not going to arrest him all by yourself, are you? You wouldn't be that daft, I hope."

Elizabeth smiled. "Don't worry, Violet. I have no intention of doing anything that silly. I'm not absolutely certain that I'm right, so I can't tell you who I think it is quite yet. But if I'm right, then everyone should know the truth by tomorrow."

"You're going to the police? The inspector, I hope. I wouldn't trust that George Dalrymple to hold onto a murderer, nor Sid Goffin, neither."

"What was it you were saying to me about worrying too much?" Elizabeth opened the door, letting in the warm sunshine of the late-August afternoon. "I promise you, I'll be careful."

She left Violet in the doorway and ran lightly down the steps. A few minutes later she was on her way down the lane toward Winnie's cottage.

She found both Winnie and Stan working in the front garden when she arrived. Both were red in the face and perspiring in the muggy heat. Winnie greeted her with a wave, while Stan wiped the sweat from his face with a large blue handkerchief.

"We're getting rid of these weeds at last," Winnie said, pointing at the wheelbarrow full of torn dandelions and thistles. "It's so good to have a man around the house again." She dropped her hoe and stepped onto the path.

"Come inside, Lady Elizabeth. I've just made some lemonade from that powder they sell at Bodkins, the grocers. At least there's still a few things we can get off ration." She glanced at her husband. "Coming in, too, Stan?"

He shook his head. "You go ahead. I want to finish here before it gets dark." He nodded at Elizabeth. "Nice of you to call, Lady Elizabeth. I want to thank you for being so kind and helpful to my wife."

"Not at all." Elizabeth gave him a smile. "I'll be attending Beryl's funeral tomorrow, of course. I just wish your return home had been under happier circumstances."

Stan looked down at his big hands resting on the handle of his garden fork. "So do I, m'm. It will be hard to go back, after this."

"I'm sure it will." Elizabeth followed Violet into the cool shadows of her living room, her heart aching for the bereaved parents. How terrible to lose a child. Especially this way. She just hoped that her plan worked. Its success wouldn't bring Beryl back, of course, but at least Winnie and Stan would have the comfort of knowing that the murderer of their daughter would be brought to justice.

With a glass of the cool lemonade in front of her, Elizabeth explained her theory, while Winnie sat perfectly still with a look of shock on her face.

"You're telling me that the man who murdered Beryl actually came into my home that night, after killing my little girl?"

"That's what I think." Elizabeth took a sip of the biting, tart drink and set it down. "Proving it might be a little difficult, but I firmly believe the murderer needed an alibi for the time Beryl was killed. He made it look as if she'd died Sunday morning, when actually she probably died some time on Saturday evening. If I'm right, he let himself into the house, rumpled her bedding to make it look as if she'd slept in it, then left again."

"And I'd taken my tablets, so I didn't hear him leave." Winnie looked dazed. "But wait a minute. How did he get into the house? I always kept everything locked up ever since they warned us about an invasion. The only way anyone could have got into this house was with a key."

"Exactly." Elizabeth folded her hands on the table. "Which is why I'm here. Did Beryl have her own key?"

"Well, of course she did, m'm. She was always coming home late. Long after I'd gone to sleep. She had to have her own key."

"Where did she keep it?"

"In her handbag, I suppose. She always had it with her."

"The handbag she left in her bicycle," Elizabeth said quietly. "Did you happen to notice if the key was missing?"

Winnie's eyes grew to enormous circles. "Come to think of it . . ." She got up abruptly from her chair and hurried into the kitchen. When she returned, Beryl's black handbag was in her hand. "I know everyone searched this," she said, opening it up, "but we were all looking for what was in here. We never gave a thought to what *wasn't* in here."

She turned the bag upside down and let the assortment of hairpins, pencils, a nail file, coins, lipsticks, and several bus ticket stubs fall onto the table. Shaking it just to make sure, she announced, "Well, there it is. No key."

"Just as I thought." Elizabeth felt a small surge of triumph. "You're quite sure?"

Winnie pulled the bag open wider and peered inside. "Quite sure, m'm. No key. That murdering bugger must have taken it. Excuse me, m'm."

"Not at all." Elizabeth sat back in her chair. "Now I think we should have a little chat."

Long after midnight that night, a shadowy figure stood poised at the garden gate of Winnie Pierce's cottage. The intruder waited, head cocked on one side, to listen in the quiet stillness of the countryside.

An owl hooted somewhere deep in the woods, and a soft breeze rustled the branches of the oak tree, sending a dappled pattern of leaves across the shuttered windows. Otherwise all was quiet in the shadowed lane.

After a moment or two, a ghostly hand reached out and unlatched the gate. The clear skies allowed the moon to light the way up the long, neat path to the cottage door. The dark-clad body bent over almost double and crept stealthily up to the porch, where he paused.

His head turned, looking this way and that, then his hand snaked out and fitted a bright, shiny key into the keyhole. A twist of the wrist, and the lock slid open with only the tiniest of clicks.

Very slowly the hand pushed on the door. It swung open silently on its well-oiled hinges. Again the intruder waited, then after several moments had ticked by, stepped cautiously inside the living room.

Leaving the door open, the dark figure trod softly across to the stairs, then began to mount them, inching up one by one. About halfway up he paused, then, re-assured, stepped onto the next stair. A soft creak startled him. At that precise moment, without a hint of warning, blazing light flooded the stairwell.

Momentarily blinded, he rubbed his eyes, then, heart thudding against his ribs, he stared up at the two figures standing at the top of the stairs.

"Good evening, Evan," Stan Pierce said in a cold, hard

voice the intruder hardly recognized. "Were you looking for something?"

Evan switched his gaze to Winnie, who stood by her husband's side, her hand gripping his arm, her face dead white against the shadows behind her.

Instinct screamed at him to run. He twisted around, all set to plunge down the stairs and out into the freedom of the night. But then he pulled up short as two burly figures appeared at the foot of the stairs.

"Going somewhere, were you, Evan?" George Dalrymple inquired. Sid Goffin merely smiled.

Just for a second Evan considered the possibility of shoving between the two elderly men, but when Lady Elizabeth stepped out of the shadows, it was just one too many to take on. Evan collapsed and sank onto the stairs. It was over.

"I can't believe you went down there last night," Violet said, dumping a soft-boiled egg down in front of Elizabeth. "What on earth were you thinking? The lady of the manor skulking around a tenant's cottage in the middle of the night waiting for a murderer to turn up. You could have been killed."

"I don't think so." Elizabeth spooned powdered milk into her tea and stirred it. "After all, apart from George and Sid, Winnie and Stan Pierce were also there. I felt confident they could handle Evan Potter. He's not that ferocious."

"You were still taking a big chance." Winnie went to the door of the kitchen and yelled, "Martin? If you want your weekly egg you'd better get to the table right now."

"Actually," Elizabeth murmured when Violet returned to the table, "I was in more danger when I went to see Evan yesterday afternoon. I mean, I was quite alone with him in the barn. I suppose, if he'd had a mind to, he could easily have attacked me there."

Violet gave a little squeak. "What on earth did you do that for?"

"I had to make my visit look plausible. If I had taken someone with me, Evan would have been immediately suspicious. As it was, I was able to set him up without him suspecting a thing. Though I must say, if he'd known Stan had arrived home yesterday, he might not have been quite so eager to fall into my little trap."

"So what did you tell him to make him go back to the cottage?"

Elizabeth smiled. "Well, I told him I'd stopped by to let him know we'd discovered the father of Beryl's baby. He didn't seem too shocked by the news. For good reason, I found out later. I also very casually mentioned that Winnie had found something on the floor of Beryl's bedroom that the police believed belonged to whoever killed her. I told Evan that Winnie was leaving the object there until the inspector came down from Norwich today to take a look at it."

"Ah." Winnie sat down at the table. "And that's when Evan decided to go back to the house to get something he thought belonged to him."

"Exactly." Elizabeth glanced up as Martin ambled into the room.

"Good morning, madam. Lovely morning out there. I've just taken a turn around the grounds."

"Looking for the cowboys' horses, I suppose," Violet mumbled as she got up.

"Horses? They're in the stables, of course." Martin sat down, then immediately stood up again. "I say, madam, I'm most terribly sorry. Do, please, beg my pardon. I'm just not accustomed to seeing you here."

"Lady Elizabeth sits at that table every blinking morning," Violet said crossly. "I don't know how many times you say the same thing."

"Yes, quite." Martin adjusted his glasses, then peered over the top of them at Elizabeth. "If you don't mind my saying so, madam, you really should be taking your meals in the dining room, where it's proper for a lady to be dining."

"I don't mind you saying so at all, Martin." Elizabeth reached for a piece of toast.

"He's right, you know." Violet placed an egg nestled in a pale blue eggcup in front of Martin's place at the table. "Sit down, Martin. You look like a bloody recruitment poster for the army, standing there all stiff like that."

"If I have your permission, madam?"

Elizabeth sighed. Every morning Martin asked her permission to be seated at the table. And every morning she gave him the same answer, to which he gave the same response. "Of course you may, Martin."

"Thank you, madam. It is a privilege to share a table with you." He settled himself on his chair, which for Martin was a major operation.

Violet carried the third egg in its eggcup over to the table and sat down with it. "There's something I don't understand," she said, picking up her knife. "How did you know it was Evan? It could have been that Yank Beryl was running around with. Or what about his girlfriend? She had plenty to be mad about. What is it they say? Hell has no fury like a woman scorned?"

"I say, Violet." Martin glared at her across the table. "I don't think we should use such vulgar words in the presence of madam."

"It's all right, Martin. Madam has been known to use

the word herself now and again," Elizabeth murmured.

Ignoring Martin's look of horror, Violet asked, "So how could you be so sure it was Evan?"

Elizabeth couldn't help feeling pleased with herself. She'd been rather clever, even if she did say so herself. She picked up her own knife and neatly sliced the cap off her egg. Then she broke off a piece of toast and dipped it into the still-runny yolk.

"It was two things, actually," she said, after enjoying her first precious bite. "Evan's mother told me that Evan didn't get along with his father, and that he always made excuses to stay out of the house. It seemed odd to me that the day after Beryl apparently had stood him up, he'd spent that entire Sunday at home. I would have thought that was one day he would have much preferred spending the day in the Tudor Arms instead of fighting with his father."

Violet uncapped her egg with the same neat flick of her knife. "That was strange, all right. But then, he could have been sick with worry and didn't want to go out."

"True. Which is what I thought at first. But then something else he said bothered me, but it wasn't until yesterday that I realized why. Evan told me that Beryl had changed lately, wearing too much makeup, dressing inappropriately, and getting her hair cut short, that sort of thing."

Martin picked up his egg spoon and began tapping on the top of his egg.

Violet glanced at him, then turned her attention back to Elizabeth. "How did that tell you he murdered her?"

"Evan said that Beryl didn't arrive for their date that evening, and that he hadn't seen her in two days. But Winnie told me that Beryl had her hair cut short that Saturday morning. There was no mention anywhere in the newspaper about Beryl's haircut, and the picture they used was an old one, when her hair was still long. Evan remained at home after her body was found, at least up until the day I talked to him. So no one could have told him about Beryl's new look. I had to ask myself, if Evan didn't see Beryl that Saturday, and no one told him about it, how did he know she'd had her hair cut?"

Martin went on tapping his egg, while Violet stared at Elizabeth. "Well, I'll be blowed! That's really clever."

"Thank you," Elizabeth said smugly. "I rather thought it was. I still had to prove my theory, however. I felt quite sure that if Evan was guilty, and thought Winnie had found something to incriminate him, he would attempt to retrieve it before the inspector could see it." Her smile faded. "I have to say, though, it was sad to see that boy break down when he was confronted last night."

"Did he say why he did it?"

Elizabeth watched Martin peel a tiny piece of shell from his egg and place it carefully on the side of his plate. "Yes, as a matter of fact, he did. Apparently he'd gone to North Horsham that afternoon on an errand and had seen Beryl talking to one of the American airmen. Evan said she was hanging on his arm, and he could tell they knew each other very well."

"So he got jealous, I bet. Can't really blame him."

"Well, Beryl, it seems, had done this sort of thing before, and something must have snapped in Evan's mind. Instead of going back to the Tudor Arms as they'd arranged, he waited for her on the coast road, determined to have it out with her in private. Beryl must have been extremely upset, since she made the mistake of telling Evan that she was having a baby and the father had refused to marry her."

"Beryl was having a baby? That poor Winnie. She's

lost not only a daughter but a grandchild as well. That's so tragic."

"Yes, it is." Elizabeth sighed. "Anyway, when Evan threatened to confront the American, and have it out with him, Beryl told him he wasn't the father. She told him the real father of her baby was a British soldier stationed in London.

Violet swallowed a piece of toast. "Oh, my, that girl certainly got around in her tea half hour, didn't she."

"Well, it was one too many betrayals for Evan, that's for sure. Especially since both men involved were in the forces. That must have been adding insult to injury in view of his bitterness about being unaccepted by the army."

"So he strangled her and threw her over the cliff." Violet shuddered. "What a terrible thing to happen."

Elizabeth glanced at Martin, concerned as to how he was taking all this talk of murder. He seemed not to be listening, however, intent on peeling the shell from his egg one tiny piece at a time.

"Evan threw the bicycle down after her," she went on, "hoping people would think that she'd fallen over. Then he went on to the Tudor Arms as if nothing had happened. He made sure everyone in the pub knew Beryl had stood him up, but he started to panic when he realized the police would probably know she'd been strangled."

"He might have known that," Violet said. She was watching Martin now, with a look of irritation on her face.

Knowing what was coming, Elizabeth nevertheless continued her story. "Anyway, Evan went back to the beach, intending to hide the body. When he got there, Beryl had disappeared, her body taken out by the tide.

The bicycle was still there, however. Evan took the key out of her handbag and went back to her house. He knew about Winnie's tablets, of course. Beryl had told him about them. He let himself in, rumpled Beryl's bed, and left again. He went straight home and stayed there for the next few days, therefore establishing a solid alibi for himself."

Violet seemed to have lost interest in the saga. She sat glaring at Martin, who was still peeling tiny pieces of shell from his egg. Finally, as Elizabeth had been expecting, her voice rapped out sharply across the table. "Martin! For Gawd's sake, why can't you use a knife to cut your blinking egg like the rest of us? By the time you get it open it'll be cold and hard as a bullet."

Martin lifted his head, spoon poised in midair. "Violet, I don't tell you how to cook the egg. Please be so kind as to refrain from telling me how to eat it."

Violet rolled her eyes and slumped back in her chair. "He'll be the death of me, I know he will."

Elizabeth laid down her spoon and reached for her tea. "Nonsense, Violet. You two thoroughly enjoy sparring with each other. Think how dull life would be without each other to add excitement to your days."

Violet snorted. "I think there's been more than enough excitement around here lately. I'm glad this nasty business is over and done with. Maybe now we can get back to normal."

"Normal." Elizabeth set her cup back in its saucer. "I don't know what is normal anymore. I have to admit, I rather enjoyed the adventure. I particularly enjoyed the challenge of hunting down clues and working out what they meant. It was all rather invigorating."

"Invigorating, maybe, but very unsuitable behavior for

the lady of the manor." Violet rose from the table. "Your mother would not approve."

Elizabeth sighed. "Maybe not. But I think Daddy might have agreed that the situation had some interesting moments."

"Well, let me tell you, I wouldn't be at all surprised if we don't have more than our share of interesting moments once them Americans move in tomorrow."

Tomorrow. Elizabeth's pulse gave a little skip. After today the Manor House would no longer be her peaceful, private domain. Tomorrow the east wing would be occupied by a group of American officers. Tomorrow, she would be living under the same roof as Major Earl Monroe.

Much as she tried to repress the thought, there was no doubt in her mind that she found the prospect every bit as intriguing and exciting as her recent venture into the dark realm of murder.